"Scared?" Tyler Murmured.

"No, it's worse than that," Carrie whispered, fighting the urge to close her eyes and give in to the sensuality of the moment. "I wish I *were* scared."

"Now, why would you wish that?" Tyler slid his hands over her, delighting in the feel of her, small and feminine, yet strong and supple.

Carrie stared at his temptingly sexy mouth, and a sensual shiver rippled up her spine. Somehow, as if of their own volition, her arms rose and her hands locked at the nape of his neck. She stood on tiptoe, pressed tightly against him, inhaling his heady male scent and relishing the hard, unyielding masculine planes of his body. It had been so long, so long. . . .

"You're making me feel things I thought I'd never feel again," she said softly, "and that's far more dangerous than being afraid of you. . . ."

Dear Reader,

Let's talk about summer—those wonderful months of June, July and August, when the weather warms up and Silhouette Desire stays hot.

June: Here is where you'll find another dynamite romance about the McLachlan brothers—this time Ross—by BJ James (look for more brothers later in the year!), a *Man of the Month* by Barbara Boswell, and another installment in the *Hawk's Way* series by Joan Johnston.

July: Don't look now but it's the *Red, White and Blue* heroes! These men are red-blooded, white-knight, blue-collar guys, and I know you'll love all of them! Look for the hero portrait on each and every one of these books.

August: It's a *Man of the Month* from Diana Palmer, a story from Dixie Browning and another delightful tale from Lass Small . . . and that's just a *tiny* amount of what's going on in August.

Yes, I think summer's going to be pretty terrific, and in the meantime I want to ask you all some questions. What do you think of the Desire line? Is there anything you'd particularly like to see that we don't provide? No answer is too outrageous; I *want* to hear your opinions.

So write and let me know. And yes, I really do exist! I'm not just some made-up name that goes on the bottom of these letters.

Until next month, happy reading,

Lucia Macro
Senior Editor

BARBARA BOSWELL
TRIPLE TREAT

SILHOUETTE *Desire*®
Published by Silhouette Books New York
America's Publisher of Contemporary Romance

SILHOUETTE BOOKS
300 East 42nd St., New York, N.Y. 10017

TRIPLE TREAT

Copyright © 1993 by Barbara Boswell

ISBN: 0-373-05787-3

First Silhouette Books printing June 1993

All the characters in this book have no existence outside the imagination of the author and have no relation whatsoever to anyone bearing the same name or names. They are not even distantly inspired by any individual known or unknown to the author, and all incidents are pure invention.

® and ™:Trademarks used with authorization. Trademarks indicated with ® are registered in the United States Patent and Trademark Office, the Canada Trade Mark Office and in other countries.

Printed in the U.S.A.

BARBARA BOSWELL

loves writing about families. "I guess family has been a big influence on my writing," she says. "I particularly enjoy writing about how my characters' family relationships affect them."

When Barbara isn't writing and reading, she's spending time with her *own* family—her husband, three daughters and three cats, who she concedes are the true bosses of their home! She has lived in Europe, but now makes her home in Pennsylvania. She collects miniatures and holiday ornaments, tries to avoid exercise and has somehow found the time to write over twenty category romances.

One

"**D**o you have any plans for the weekend?" Cole Tremaine asked his brother Tyler as they emerged from the air-conditioned chill of the office building into the warmth of the sunny May day.

Tyler immediately donned his mirrored sunglasses against the brightness. "This is Memorial Day weekend," he explained patiently.

"Ah, say no more." Cole grinned. "How could I have forgotten, even for a moment? Memorial Day weekend is Tyler Tremaine's bacchanalian kickoff to the summer social season. What began as a simple cookout ten years ago has evolved into a—"

"Enough!" Tyler held up his hand, his lips tightening into a world-weary grimace. "I just heard this lecture from Dad and I don't care to hear it from you, too, big brother."

"Exactly which lecture would this be?" Cole asked amusedly.

"The one about me turning thirty-five last month and still showing no signs of settling down with a—quote—nice, suitable young woman—unquote—who will turn me into a serious-minded, devoted family man."

"Nice, suitable young woman, hmm?" Cole hid a smile. "Do you suppose Dad has anyone in particular in mind? Somebody's wellborn, well-connected, eligible daughter or niece, perhaps?"

"Undoubtedly, but he didn't mention any names. He did mention that he's certain this nice, suitable young woman couldn't possibly be one of my current acquaintances. Dad thinks every woman I date is either a bimbo or a gold-digger or a combination thereof."

Cole chuckled. "Gee, I wonder where he ever got that impression?"

"Don't you start in on me, too! The simple truth is that I'm not interested in settling down with a *nice, suitable young woman*—at least, not for a long, long time. I mean, what's the rush? Men in their fifties are able to have children and get married and—"

"Ah, the Warren Beatty defense," Cole said, nodding. "Certainly a compelling argument for extended bachelorhood. I trust you made use of it during your talk with Dad. Was he at all swayed?"

"Not a bit. Said he doesn't care what anybody else does, that *I'm* his son and he can't stand to watch me waste the best years of my life with a parade of meaningless women and activities...." Tyler's voice trailed off. "You get the picture, I'm sure. He probably gave you the same lecture before you married Chelsea."

"No, he didn't. Dad's changed a lot in the past few years, Tyler," Cole said thoughtfully. "Ever since he married Nina he—"

"—wants everybody else in the universe to be tied down, too," Tyler interrupted glumly. "Misery loves company, I suppose."

"Dad is not miserable, and you know it. He's been walking on air since he married Nina, and I don't think he's hit the ground yet. He really wants his sons to be as happy as he is. And Dad does make a valid point about not wasting years of your life chasing after everything except what will bring you true happiness. He loved Nina for—how long was it? almost thirty-five years?—before he finally—"

"I don't want to talk about the star-crossed love story of Dad and Nina," Tyler cut in roughly. "It has nothing to do with me. I'm not carrying a torch for anyone. I'm perfectly happy with my life exactly the way it is and I damn well resent being told that I'm wasting my time because I choose not to chain myself to some *nice, suitable young woman* who will dutifully provide me with the requisite heir and proceed to turn me into some kind of domestic paragon."

"It would take more than a nice, suitable young woman to accomplish that," Cole said jovially. "You'd need something along the lines of a miracle worker to pull off such a stunning transformation."

"Funny, Cole." Tyler's smile more closely resembled a wolf baring his teeth than a grin of mirth. "Keep those jokes coming. They're just what I need after a half hour of Dad's ranting and raving about the joys and respectability of domestic bliss."

"Sorry," Cole replied, though he did not sound even slightly apologetic. "I'll drop the subject of your—er—social life and move on to safer ground. Something like real estate, maybe?"

Tyler groaned. "Safer ground...real estate.... Yet another one of your truly atrocious attempts at humor. My advice is to keep your day job at Tremaine Incorporated and stay away from stand-up comedy, brother."

"Okay, I'll spare you any more of my devastating wit. I do have a grounds-related question, though. Have you had any luck buying the corner lot next door to your place? A while ago, you mentioned that the old man who lived there was dying and that you were going to make him an offer for his property that he couldn't refuse. Whatever happened with that?''

Tyler frowned. ''Unfortunately, nothing happened. My lawyer finally got in to see the old recluse and made him that offer, which he had absolutely no trouble refusing. He died shortly afterward and left the place to his nephew.''

''And the nephew's asking price soared the moment he learned that a Tremaine was interested in buying the property,'' Cole surmised. ''Too bad, Tyler.''

''The nephew is dead, so his widow and children inherited the place,'' Tyler said flatly, ''and apparently, they intend to live there. They moved in about three months ago.''

''Well, I hope you're not entertaining any nefarious plans to make them sell to you,'' Cole said sternly. ''I mean, intimidating widows and orphans is not—''

''I haven't intimidated the widow,'' Tyler cut in with a long-suffering sigh. ''In fact, I've been downright civil to her. Over the phone, that is. I haven't met her in person.''

''You called her?''

''She called me last month before I left for Japan on that marketing trip. She'd found this miserable-looking tabby cat skulking around in her cellar and thought it might be mine. The cat is a stray—I call him Psycho-Kitty because of his less than amiable personality—and I'd been leaving food out for him, but I assured her that he was definitely not my cat. She decided to let him move in with them.''

Tyler smiled slightly. ''She said she'd named him Sleuth because he can find his way in and out of anywhere without being detected. Sleuth! I told her it was the stupidest name for a cat I'd ever heard and that she was nuts to let him inside her house.''

''You told her she was stupid and crazy, hmm?'' Cole arched his dark brows. ''Is that what you call being downright civil or is it a sample of your much heralded charm?''

"I was doing her a favor. I had valid reasons for naming that cat Psycho-Kitty—he's as unpredictable as a terrorist. Anyway, I'm not trying to charm Carrie—that's her name, Carrie Wilcox. I want to get her off the property so I can buy it, not bowl her over with neighborly friendliness."

"Well, this weekend brawl you call a picnic might just do the trick," said Cole. "If the poor widow has lived next door to you for only three months, then this will be her first experience with the way you entertain your many, many, *many* friends. It's sure to be an appalling surprise. I feel sorry for the unfortunate woman."

"I'm going to invite her to the party," Tyler said, smiling wickedly. Behind his mirrored sunglasses, his green eyes were gleaming with purpose. "I'll stop by her place as soon as I get home. I always invite my neighbors to my parties— the homeowners, that is. I don't bother with the transient apartment dwellers."

"I assume your neighbors never come, but inviting them is sort of an insurance policy against having them call the police to complain about the noise and all those zesty antics that go on until all hours?"

Tyler nodded. "It makes them feel like mean-spirited killjoys, calling the cops on a party they were invited to."

"Wonder how the widow will react?" mused Cole. "She has kids, you say? How many? Hold old are they?"

"How am I supposed to know?" growled Tyler. "Do I look like the welcoming committee? I didn't call on the Wilcoxes when they moved in, and I've been in Japan for the past month. This afternoon will be the first time I've set foot in the place since I went over to pay my last respects to old Mr. Wilcox."

"And make a final bid for his property," added Cole.

"Which was turned down flat by his lawyer." Tyler frowned, then brightened. "Well, maybe after this weekend Mrs. Wilcox and her brood will be more receptive to my offer to buy them out."

"I think you can count on it," Cole said wryly. He glanced at his watch. "I'd better get home. Chelsea and I are taking the children up to the cabin in the Catoctin Mountains this weekend. We want to leave right after dinner so the kids will be asleep during most of the drive."

"A car trip with two kids—now, that's the stuff of nightmares." Tyler shuddered. "Why bother going anywhere with small children? No matter where you go, it's the same routine of looking after them every minute of the day and night. You might as well stay at home—at least it saves you the trouble of carting their unlimited paraphernalia from place to place."

"I don't think this is the time or place for me to go into the joys of parenthood with you, Tyler," Cole said dryly. "So I'll just say that someday you'll understand and appreciate the role of children in your life."

"More threats." Tyler flashed his white, straight teeth. "This seems to be the day for them. First Dad with his 'nice, suitable young woman' curse, now you with the menacing 'wait until you have kids of your own' hex. Well, I'm going to celebrate the absence of both in my life by thoroughly enjoying every moment of the holiday weekend."

The brothers parted, laughing and wishing each other a good weekend, despite the disparity of their plans. Cole headed to his comfortable suburban Maryland home where his wife, Chelsea, three-year-old Daniel and ten-month-old Kylie Ann eagerly awaited him.

Tyler drove to his neighborhood in a once fashionable but now aging residential section of northwest Washington, D.C. There were yards and trees and shabbily kept, genteel houses, most of which needed large infusions of cash to restore them to their former glory. Many longtime residents of the street spent their winters and summers elsewhere, letting their property fall into slow decline. After the deaths of some elderly neighbors, their houses were sold and divided into apartments, a lucrative bonus for the heirs, who already had homes and lives elsewhere. Young people, many of them new to the D.C. area, single or recently divorced, in graduate schools or entry-level government jobs, moved in and out of the apartments without anybody really noticing that they'd come or gone.

If there had ever been a cohesive sense of neighborhood, it was already gone by the time Tyler had moved onto the street ten years ago. He didn't mind; the impersonal, increasingly transitional atmosphere of the area suited him. He had no need for neighborhood block parties or Block Watch or Block Parents or any other programs that would provide the street with a communal, protective air.

He owned a three-story brick house perched in the middle of a spacious tree-lined yard, next door to a small frame house on the desirable corner lot. From the time he'd moved in, Tyler had planned to buy that corner lot and tear down the ugly little house on it, thus considerably extending his territory. So far he'd had no luck, but he was certain that he would prevail. It was inevitable; there had never been a Tremaine who didn't get what he wanted, eventually.

Tyler swung his car, a red 1957 Thunderbird convertible, the crown jewel in his classic car collection, into the narrow driveway of the run-down little house next door to his. He might as well extend his invitation to the widow and her offspring in person. Still wearing his corporate executive attire of gray suit, immaculate white shirt and red power tie, he strode to the front door and sounded the tarnished brass knocker.

The door was opened a few moments later by a tall, blond young man in cutoff jeans and a tank top, whose age Tyler guessed to be about twenty. Obviously the son of the widow, Tyler decided. He'd imagined the woman to be fifty-something, and a college-age son fit the scenario.

"I'm your next-door neighbor, Tyler Tremaine," he said, flashing his best friendly neighbor grin.

To make himself seem 'less formidable and more approachable, he removed his suit coat, unfastened the top buttons of his shirt and loosened his tie as he spoke. He also felt considerably cooler. It seemed that the high temperature for the day had been reached on this airless, covered porch.

"I'd like to invite you and your whole family to my annual Memorial Day picnic tomorrow. It's a tradition of mine to invite the entire neighborhood. We'll start serving dinner around nine, but feel free to drop by earlier for drinks and snacks if you'd like. The most indefatigable early birds generally start showing up around seven."

The young man stared at him, seemingly stunned. Finally he collected himself enough to offer his hand for an introductory shake. "Come in, come in, please. I'm Ben Shaw, Carrie's brother. Thank-you for inviting us to your party."

Tyler stepped inside and took a quick glance around. The vestibule where they stood, and the two rooms visible from there, revealed faded wallpaper, aging fixtures, ruinously scuffed floors and windows that were little more than decaying relics. The place was a dump, and restoration would cost a mint. The widow and her family would be better off living elsewhere on the tidy sum they would receive for this property, Tyler decided loftily.

Ben Shaw took a deep breath, as if to bolster himself. "You...wouldn't happen to be one of *the* Tremaines, would you? The—the ones who own the drugstore and bookstore chains?"

Tyler smiled graciously. He was accustomed to the awed reactions of those who connected him to the family company's phenomenally successful chain of area discount drugstores and fast-growing national chain of bookstores.

"I plead guilty," he said politely. He reached into the pocket of his coat and removed one of his business cards that identified him as Tyler Tremaine, Executive Vice-

President, Marketing and Public Affairs, Tremaine Incorporated.

Ben studied the card reverentially, then slipped it into the pocket of his cutoff jeans. "It's an honor to meet you, sir," he said, his tone worshipfully hushed.

Tyler felt a mild streak of annoyance. *Sir?* He wasn't that much older than the kid! But standing here before this respectful young man was beginning to make him feel middle-aged or something. Tyler did not care for the feeling.

"I know my sister will want to ask Mrs. Tremaine if there is anything she can bring to the picnic," Ben continued politely. "Carrie makes this terrific pudding thing with marshmallows and fruit that she could—"

Tyler stared at him. Marshmallow pudding? At his orgiastic saturnalia? "That won't be necessary," he said quickly. "And there isn't a Mrs. Tremaine. That is, not a Mrs. *Tyler* Tremaine. The three current Mrs. Tremaines belong to my father and, uh, two brothers, respectively."

"You haven't bitten the bullet and taken the vows yet, huh? Me, either," Ben confided fraternally. "And frankly, I'm not in any hurry."

Tyler shifted uncomfortably. He did not want to swap confidences with this youngster. And suddenly, in the midst of his discomfiture, a realization struck. "You said you're Carrie's brother? Would that be Carrie Wilcox, the—er—widow who inherited this place from old Mr. Wilcox?" Something didn't compute here. Could a fifty-something widow have a college student for a brother?

"Yeah, that's my sister and she—" Ben cut himself off, turning abruptly to yell, "Hey, Carrie, you've got company!"

Tyler heard the voice before he saw the woman. "Benjy, sshh! You'll wake the baby!" The tone was admonishing but it was the same husky, slightly girlish voice he'd conversed with over the phone.

Ben shrugged and looked sheepish. "Carrie, this is your neighbor, Ty—"

"Oh, Mr. Tyler!" Carrie Shaw Wilcox appeared in the small hallway. "It's so nice to meet you at last." She came right up to Tyler and took his hand in hers in a firmly gentle shake, smiling up at him, her wide-set blue eyes shining with warmth. "Have you come to check on Sleuth? He's doing fine. He made a quick adjustment to life as an indoor cat."

Her voice swirled around Tyler's head and he heard the words, something about the cat, but he wasn't really comprehending them. He stared at her in total confusion for she was clearly not the fiftyish widow he'd been expecting. Carrie Wilcox looked as young as her brother, maybe younger—*a teenage widow?*—and she was strikingly pretty, small-boned with a heart-shaped face and delicate features.

His eyes swept over her pale blond hair, which swung thick and straight around her shoulders. She was petite, about five foot three, and she appeared all but dwarfed between him and her brother. She had ocean-blue eyes that were framed with long, dark lashes, and when she smiled, her whole face seemed to light with pleasure. She was wearing loose-fitting blue-and-white-striped shorts and a matching crop top, and though her clothes were certainly modest enough, Tyler was startlingly aware of her slender but shapely nubile young body. Her skin was clear and smooth and looked soft to the touch.

Tyler took an instinctive step backward and had to remind himself to breathe. So this is what it felt like to be struck by a lightning bolt?

"Carrie, his name isn't Mr. Tyler, it's Tremaine," brother Ben informed his sister urgently. "You know, Tremaine Drugs and Tremaine Books. *That* Tremaine."

Carrie looked confused. "I thought he said his name was Mr. Something Tyler when we talked on the ph—"

"No, you must've heard him wrong. He's Tyler *Tremaine*," Ben insisted. "I have his business card to prove it. Want to see?"

It occurred to Tyler that they were discussing him between themselves as if he were invisible. He cleared his throat. It was definitely time to assert his presence. "Perhaps we had a bad connection that night, uh, Mrs. Wilcox. You caught the Tyler but not the Tremaine."

"A bad connection from next door?" Carrie laughed. "You're very tactful, Mr. Tremaine."

"Please, as we're neighbors, I insist that you call me Tyler, Mrs. Wilcox."

She tilted her head and looked at him, those big blue eyes of hers dancing with amusement. "That sounds like a cue for me to insist that you call me Carrie."

"It was and I will, Carrie."

Tyler studied her curiously. She was much too young for him, of course, and she'd mentioned a baby, therefore canceling any chances she might've had with him even if he'd chosen to overlook her tender years. But she was a pleasure to look at, lovely and natural with a wholesome freshness he rarely saw in his sophisticated life in the fast lane. He couldn't take his eyes off her.

"You're—not at all what I expected," Tyler blurted out, surprising himself by actually speaking his thoughts aloud. Although he appeared to be the soul of spontaneity—he'd often been described that way by Tremaine friends and admirers—all those ingenuous remarks and impetuous, capricious deeds of his were actually quite premeditated, calculated and studied for their maximum effect.

He was disconcerted by his slip. "I assumed you were much older, uh, that is, with you being a widow and all." Tyler nearly groaned aloud at his lack of finesse. At this particular moment, no one could accuse him of being a silver-tongued snake, an alternate description of him offered by Tremaine enemies and detractors.

"There are widows in their twenties," Carrie said bleakly, and the light went out of her eyes. "Not too many of us, but we do exist."

He wouldn't have been surprised if she'd told him she was nineteen or younger; he was half expecting it. But sad and unsmiling, she suddenly appeared older. "How old are you?" Tyler asked and immediately smote himself for the question. He well knew how touchy women could be about their ages, regardless of age!

"We're twenty-six," Ben piped up. "Our birthday was April Fool's Day. Stupid day for a birthday, huh? You wouldn't believe the cornball jokes and gags that go with that one."

"Yes, I would because it happens to be my birthday, too." Tyler stared from brother to sister with genuine surprise. They all shared the same birthday? "And you're twins?"

"Actually, there are three of us," Carrie said. "Our sister—Alexa—and Ben and me. We're triplets." She waited for the double take that invariably accompanied that revelation.

Tyler supplied it. "Triplets?" he repeated incredulously. One didn't run across triplet siblings every day. The situation seemed to require some sort of comment from him, but nothing clever or memorable came to mind. A rarity for him. Being silver-tongued, glib and flippant quips usually came quite naturally to him.

"Our dad thought the doctor was playing an April Fool's Day joke on him when he said Mom had triplets," Ben said jocularly. "They'd been expecting twins, but Carrie here was a total surprise." Ben nudged her in the midriff with his elbow, his blue eyes teasing. "I used to say she was a total shock, but she took offense. She'd rather be surprising than shocking, although she's often both."

Carrie rolled her eyes heavenward. "Ben's the funny one in the family."

"Yeah, I can tell," Tyler said dryly. "His jokes are on a par with my brother's—and that's sub-par. Do you all live here together?"

"No, Alexa and I have our own places, but we're over here a lot," said Ben. "Uh, do you still want all of us to come to your party, or is it limited strictly to people who live in the neighborhood full-time?"

"Ben, for heaven's sakes!" admonished Carrie.

"He came over to invite us to his neighborhood Memorial Day picnic tomorrow, Carrie," countered Ben, "and he mentioned the whole family, so I was just making sure—"

"You're all invited, of course," Tyler cut in. It was disconcerting the way the two of them tended to conduct their own conversation around him, as if he was totally superfluous. Tyler Tremaine was accustomed to commanding center stage; being rendered superfluous was new to him.

He was beginning to feel strangely frazzled. And it was so warm in there!

Suddenly terribly restless, he decided that he had to leave at once. "It's getting late," he said, glancing at his watch while already backing out the door. "I've—"

"Do you want to see Sleuth before you go?" Carrie asked politely.

"That crazy cat!" exclaimed Ben. "Wait till you see his favorite hangout, Tyler!" He clasped his fingers around Tyler's forearm and gave an eager pull. "Come on."

Tyler went reluctantly into the shabby, sparsely furnished living room. Through the decrepit window, he saw the scraggly hedge that separated his property from theirs. The size and proximity of his house blocked the sunlight, casting the living room into shadows.

"There's Sleuth, on top of the breakfront," said Carrie, pointing. A fat, darkly striped cat, his left ear torn and raggedy, doubtless a souvenir from some past feline war, sat atop a heavy wooden piece in the corner of the room.

"We call it his watchtower. He also sits on top of the cabinets in the kitchen. It's like he's on guard duty," joked Ben.

"Sleuth knows and sees all," Carrie chimed in, and they both chuckled.

They were obviously enjoying a bit of shared sibling humor. Tyler felt excluded and even more anxious to leave. When the sudden wail of a baby pierced the air, he made a speedy beeline to the door. He was not about to be dragged upstairs to admire any infant!

"If you decide to come to the picnic, I'll see you tomorrow," he called as he strode briskly down the walk to his car. He was aware that he sounded as if he didn't care if they came or not. And he didn't.

Tyler snatched his handkerchief from his pocket and wiped his brow. Actually, he did care, he acknowledged grimly. He knew what they would see and hear if they came to what his brother had so accurately described as "the bacchanalian kickoff to summer," and he knew that he didn't want them to witness it. Though he considered himself jaded and cynical, he felt an uncharacteristic urge to protect Carrie and her brother because they seemed so naive and young and guileless.

Offering a pudding confection! Dragging him in to see their cat! How hopelessly unsophisticated! Their openness, their innocence, made him feel uncomfortable—and guilty, too. He was so very far out of their league; it was like Dracula meeting the Brady Bunch.

Tyler hated feeling uncomfortable and guilty as much as he disliked feeling superfluous. Carrie Shaw Wilcox and her kin had evoked all these powerful, negative feelings within him. The sooner he bought her property and got her out of there, the better. And if tomorrow's party resulted in that end . . . well, it was regrettable but necessary. The end justifies the means; wasn't that the successful marketing executive's anthem?

From the air-conditioned coolness of his bright, spacious living room, Tyler glanced down at the dilapidated frame house next door. Without warning came the sharp memory of the electrical jolt he'd felt when he caught his first glimpse of Carrie Wilcox. Just imagining her enormous dark blue eyes and heart-melting smile caused him to freeze in place.

It was unthinkable, absurd. He could not be attracted to her, he assured himself. She'd simply caught him off guard because she was so different from the women he usually met.

He *would not* be attracted to her, Tyler vowed fiercely. It was pointless and unfair... to her. He was not in the market for a sweet, unspoiled, young widowed mother; such a prospect was as unnerving as the nice, suitable young woman of his father's threats. Both types were to be dodged.

And Tyler, that artful dodger, had long ago made himself a pledge to stay free, uninvolved and unencumbered. He had never had any difficulty keeping to his oath in the past. He expected no trouble now.

Two

Carrie rushed up the stairs to retrieve eighteen-month-old Franklin from his crib. He stopped crying the moment she entered the room, and began to jump up and down, holding onto the bars, a beatific smile lighting his small face.

"Hi, Frankie, hi!" Carried greeted him gaily, lifting him from the crib and carrying him to the changing table in the corner of the room. The baby began to wriggle and kick, laughing and yelling, "Hi, hi, hi."

After a bit of a wrestling match, with a can of baby powder and package of baby wipes being flung enthusiastically to the floor by an increasingly wild Franklin, Carrie finished diapering him and tackled the job of dressing him. She didn't set her sights too high—a one-piece blue cotton sunsuit was the quickest and easiest garment to get him into. The unique and adorable—and more complicated—little outfits remained on their hangers in the closet.

"So, Mr. Sleepyhead finally decided to wake up!" Alexa Shaw appeared in the doorway, holding one toddler in her arms and another by the hand. "I needed a break from all the fun we were having outside," she confessed, setting one baby to the floor and releasing the other's hand.

The two toddlers ran into the room and headed straight to the long shelves that lined one wall of the room. Joined by Franklin, the three began to gleefully toss the neatly ordered toys to the floor.

Alexa sank into the rocking chair and heaved a tired sigh. "Dylan must've tried to dash through that break in the hedge out back at least forty times. And every time I ran to fetch him, Emily would head straight for the impatiens you planted yesterday. They're not looking too good, by the way. I sent Ben out to try and revive them."

Carrie dropped to the floor, cross-legged. Little Emily ran over and plopped herself down onto her mother's lap. She sat still long enough for Carrie to give her a hug and a kiss on the top of her blond head, then wriggled out of her mother's embrace and returned to her brothers and their mutual project of emptying the shelves.

"They never stop moving," Alexa marveled wearily. "If they aren't sleeping, they're zooming around like Siamese cats on speed."

"Mom says we were the same way at this age," said Carrie. "A triple threat, as Dad always said."

"And Mom would immediately counter with 'triple treat,'" recalled Alexa with a reminiscent smile.

The sisters watched as Dylan climbed into a child-size molded plastic chair. Franklin and Emily clambered over him, and momentarily all three were sitting on top of each other. They babbled among themselves, and then Dylan pushed the other two off and stood up, toppling the chair over, knocking them all off balance. All three went sprawling to the floor.

Both Carrie and Alexa rose to go to their aid, but the intrepid trio picked themselves up and scampered over to the enormous stuffed panda bear that sat under the window.

Laughing boisterously, they threw themselves onto the panda's soft, plush body.

"Ben was totally hyped-up about an invitation to a picnic next door tomorrow," said Alexa as she and Carrie watched the children play. "Do you know anything about it?"

Carrie nodded. "My next-door neighbor, Tyler Tremaine, just dropped by to invite all of us to his picnic tomorrow. It sounds like a neighborhood get-together, so I'd like to go and finally meet some of the neighbors. Will you come with us, Lex? I could really use your help with the babies."

"You're not actually going to eat dinner over there with the kids, are you?" Alexa asked incredulously.

Carrie laughed. "Of course not. You've seen what mealtimes are like with these three. We'd scare the neighbors away and send poor Mr. Tremaine into a state of catatonic shock. He looks like the precise, fastidious type—you know, neat, unwrinkled and immaculate, even when he's sweating. I'm sure his house is frighteningly orderly."

"A two-minute visit by the manic Wilcox triplets will put an end to that," joked Alexa.

"That's about as long as I plan to stay," said Carrie. "I thought I'd take them over after dinner, stay outside in the yard while we're introduced to some of the neighbors, and then come home. You know, put in a polite appearance."

"I guess I can tolerate that much socializing. And you *will* need help with the kids." Alexa appeared to be trying to talk herself into the outing. "Why is Ben so all-fired eager to go? A neighborhood picnic is pretty lame by his standards, isn't it?"

"Ben is so wildly impressed by the name Tremaine he'd go to a nuclear fallout site if one of them asked him to," Carrie said dryly. "He all but bowed and scraped and paid homage to Tyler Tremaine the whole time he was over here."

"Wait a minute," cried Alexa. "*Tremaine*. As in the Tremaine wing at the Hospital Center? As in Tremaine Drugs and Tremaine Books? The zillionaires who are always giving grants and donating things and doing all sorts of other philanthropic deeds? *Those* Tremaines?"

"The very same. I could almost see the wheels turning in Ben's busy little mind." Carrie grimaced knowingly. "And it was all about cultivating Tyler Tremaine's friendship and landing the Tremaine account for the ad agency."

"The agency would certainly give him a private office of his own if he pulled that off," observed Alexa. "No more cubicle by the men's room for Benjamin Shaw if he were to land the Tremaine account."

"Sometimes Ben's ambition worries me," confessed Carrie. "He can be so calculating and manipulative. I almost felt like I ought to warn Tyler Tremaine to be on his guard. After all, he came over here in good faith to invite us to his party. He shouldn't have to put up with being hustled by an aspiring advertising shark, even if it is our own Ben."

"I'm sure Tyler Tremaine can take care of himself, Carrie. A man in his position must learn how to spot and deal with potential users at a fairly young age. What's he like, anyway?"

Carrie stared into space, remembering. "He looked to be in his mid-thirties, and he's a couple inches taller than Ben, so that would make him about six feet one. Dark hair, green eyes that are sort of an olive color. I've never seen such an unusual shade. Classic features. A smile so potent it almost knocks you off your feet. Muscular and strong but not overbuilt like some steroid freak. Hmm, what else can I say? He's absolutely gorgeous, your basic Greek god come to life. Not that I noticed, of course."

"Of course." Alexa laughed. "Was there a single detail about him that you missed?"

Carrie shook her head. "I also noticed that he couldn't wait to leave and that he thought Ben and I were two hopelessly tacky idiots. I'm sure it pains him to think that we're right next door."

"Maybe he'll offer to buy this place," Alexa said hopefully. "Keeping in mind his vast wealth, you can demand an outrageous price, sell this dump and move into a nice neighborhood near a good school, where there are other young families with kids for the triplets to play with and—"

"Even if he were to offer, I wouldn't sell, not yet." Carrie sighed. "I can't move the children again, Alexa. We've moved too often. I want them to have some sense of stability, to stay in one place long enough to feel secure."

"Well, maybe living next door to Mr. Wonderful will have its own unexpected rewards," Alexa said thoughtfully. "You're so pretty, Carrie. Tremaine had to have noticed. Maybe he'll ask you out and—"

"Alexa, a man like Tyler Tremaine can date models and princesses and movie stars. Why on earth would he want to bother with a widow who's raising triplets? Anyway, you know how I feel about dating. I don't have the time for it, and even if I did, I'm just too tired to even consider it. Besides, what would be the point? I'll never love anybody the way I loved Ian."

"I know." Alexa reached over to squeeze her sister's shoulder. "Ian was the most wonderful man in the world, Carrie. I'll always love him as the world's best brother-in-law and as my dear friend. Oh, Carrie, if only—"

"Go!" Dylan tore across the room. "Go, go!" He headed out the door and into the hall, Emily and Franklin in hot pursuit.

"Dylan's favorite word, not to mention his favorite activity. Taking off," noted Carrie. She and Alexa jumped to their feet to follow.

Carrie was glad of the diversion. Talking about Ian was always difficult, and if Alexa were to start crying as she often did when speaking of Ian and that fateful night...

Carrie determinedly put the tragedy from her mind. She had three small children to care for and to live for—and to run after right now! They must always come first, ahead of her own thoughts and needs, ahead of her own pain. They were a living legacy of the love she and Ian had shared.

And with such a vital, active triple legacy to tend, Carrie had neither the time nor the energy nor the inclination to seek the attentions of another man. She couldn't even summon the interest to seek a date to a movie.

She had accepted her fate on the day she had kissed her beloved husband, Ian, for the last time, moments before the lid of his casket was closed forever. Though it had been tragically brief, she considered herself blessed to have found love with a man like Ian Wilcox. She'd had her chance at love, and now it was over. Carrie was certain that she could not, would not, ever love again.

"Hey, Tyler, come here! You've *got* to see this!"

Tyler was trading unveiled sexual innuendos with a well-built redhead who'd introduced herself as Rhandee, when he was summoned by Luke Minteer, a relative newcomer to his ever-widening circle. Luke was the chief administrative aide to his wholesome, upright, married congressman brother, in whose footsteps he did not care to follow. It hadn't taken new-bachelor-in-town Luke Minteer long to hook up with Tyler's fast lane crowd.

"Wait here, darling." Tyler lifted Rhandee's hand to his lips for a caressive kiss on her fingertips. She stared at him, dazed and charmed, as he'd known she would be.

The front door was propped open, and Tyler joined Luke on the wide wooden porch. "I thought this was something you shouldn't miss, Tyler," Luke said, laughing. "Take a look at what's coming up the walk."

Tyler squinted against the evening sun to see the procession moving through the front gate. He recognized Ben Shaw and his sister Carrie immediately. A tall blonde, undoubtedly the third triplet, was with them, and Carrie was pulling a red wagon which contained . . .

Tyler gaped at the sight. There were three—*three!*—tow-headed toddlers aboard, all dressed in red, white and blue sunsuits, all sporting bowl-type haircuts, all looking astonishingly similar and unmistakably the same age.

"They must've made a wrong turn on their way to the playground," chortled Luke. "A really wrong turn to end up here!"

"Hi, Tyler!" Ben called at that moment.

Carrie, pulling the wagon with one hand, raised her other hand in an uncertain wave of greeting.

"Are you sure we were invited to this?" Alexa murmured. "They're staring at us like we're mutants from another planet."

Tyler stepped off the porch and walked toward the group, Luke at his heels. "Do you know them?" Luke whispered incredulously. "Tyler, you're not going to let them in, are you? I mean, this is definitely *not* a children's party!"

Tyler's gaze was fixed on Carrie Wilcox, who looked cool and fresh and incredibly lovely in a pink-and-white candy-striped sundress and slim sandals. His eyes darted to the red wagon behind her, filled with the squirming toddlers. "They're not—" he began. He cleared his throat and tried again "—all yours?"

"Yes, they are." Carrie smiled at his expression. He couldn't have looked more shocked if she'd shown up with a wagon full of live rattlesnakes. "Dylan, Emily and Franklin. They'll be eighteen months old tomorrow."

"Triplets?" Tyler was stunned. "*Another* set of triplets?"

"Multiple births run in our family," Ben said cheerfully. "All the way back to our great-grandmother, every woman in our family has had twins or triplets. Some genetic thing, we're told. Makes me glad I'm a guy, that's for sure!"

"Kids coming in twos and threes! It's like a—a curse or something!" exclaimed Luke, backing away from them as if they were some sort of infectious agents.

Tyler found that he did not share Luke's aversion. "That's fascinating," he said, coming to a stop directly in front of Carrie. "Has it been documented?"

"Sure has! Our family has been the focus of two separate university studies," Ben boasted. "Did you happen to note our names? Alexa, Ben and Carrie—*A, B, C.* That was our birth order, and the letters were on our hospital bracelets, so our folks decided to stick with them when naming us. Carrie's kids were Babies *A, B* and *C,* too, but I convinced her to move along to the letters *D, E* and *F* for their names."

"And in a weak moment, I went along with him," Carrie said wryly.

"Must've been temporary lack of oxygen and loss of blood after giving birth to triplets," Alexa suggested drolly.

"Oh, God!" yelped Luke. He beat an immediate retreat into the house without another word or a single look backward.

Tyler shrugged. "I guess the subject of childbirth makes him queasy." Surprisingly, he felt no urge to make a similar speedy exit. Instead, he stayed where he was, standing close to Carrie. When he inhaled, he could smell the light, tantalizing scent of her perfume. For a moment, his mind seemed to cloud.

"You haven't met our sister Alexa yet," said the ever-chatty Ben. "Alexa, this is Tyler Tremaine." He spoke the name reverently.

"It's a pleasure to meet you." Tyler nodded at Alexa. She was blond and slim, about five foot seven and very attractive, but she interested him as little as Ben did. It was Carrie that he wanted to look at, wanted to talk to, though he was well aware that he shouldn't attempt to prolong their visit.

"Shall we move this traveling circus inside?" Ben suggested eagerly.

"No!" Both Tyler and Carrie exclaimed at the same time.

Now, how was he going to explain that outburst? Tyler combed his fingers through his hair in a rare, nervous gesture. "It's just that—" he began, then paused, flummoxed. It was just that he didn't dare let them inside, not with the party already heating up. And if parties were rated the way movies were, this particular party, at the early hour of 7:03, would've already earned an eye-popping NC-17. The X rating would be earned by nine or ten.

But how to tactfully explain? It was a daunting challenge, even to Tremaine Incorporated's silver-tongued king of marketing. It seemed as though he had been rendered temporarily speechless.

Carrie was the one to fill the awkward silence. "Don't worry. I understand." She appeared amused rather than insulted. "I'm sure your house isn't childproofed, and you don't want these three launching a commando raid on it. Actually, we can't stay. We just dropped over to say hello and—"

"You're very gracious, and I feel like an idiot," Tyler cut in, feeling as gauche and foolish as a bumbling adolescent. It was a first, for he'd never been a bumbling adolescent— he had been a smooth operator since childhood, when he'd realized the power of his natural smile-and-charm style.

He tried to summon that power now, flashing a smile warm enough to melt polar ice caps. "You see, there is a—"

He never had the chance to invent a polite reason for barring them from entering his home. The baby triplets, growing bored with the inactivity, launched their own escape. All three scrambled out of the wagon and took off at breakneck speed in three different directions.

Alexa, Ben and Carrie immediately sprang into action. Ben ran after Franklin who was headed toward the backyard, Alexa followed Dylan who was racing to the front door, and Carrie chased after Emily who laughingly charged toward the street.

Tyler followed Carrie and quickly outdistanced her, bending down to scoop up little Emily before she reached the sidewalk. She let out an indignant howl of protest, then stared up at him, her big blue eyes curious. It suddenly seemed to occur to her that she did not know her captor, and her expression turned wary. "Down," she said uncertainly.

"Not a chance," said Tyler. "You're up and you're going to stay up, you little monkey."

"Monk-mey," Emily repeated, and then demanded forcefully, "Down!" She arched her back and squirmed, so wriggly and rubbery that Tyler nearly lost his hold on her. Fortunately, he managed to retain his grip as the baby hung practically upside down, still in constant motion.

"I'll take her." Carrie reached for her daughter, successfully suppressing her smile of amusement. Poor Tyler looked hilariously awkward, trying to cope with Emily's acrobatics. Clearly, he'd never held an active toddler before.

Tyler gratefully handed Carrie the wriggling little girl. "Thank you for catching her," she said warmly. "You were amazingly fast."

A car roared down the street, well past the speed limit. Though Tyler had the baby in his arms well before the car had appeared, the very thought of an uncomprehending toddler dashing into a car's path shook him.

"She's the fast one—they all move at the speed of light!" Tyler drew an unsteady breath. "How do you manage with *three* of them?"

"Well, since I'm hopelessly outnumbered, I never go anywhere alone with them." Carrie laughed. "I'm not even going to try, until they're at least three years old."

"I think I'd make that age ten," said Tyler, with feeling. "Where are the other two? I don't even see—" He broke off abruptly. Since they were nowhere in sight, he had to assume that one had actually made it into the house and the other was somewhere in the backyard. In the vicinity of the pool.

Tyler groaned his dismay. "Uh-oh."

At that moment, Alexa came running out the front door, clutching a squirming Dylan on her hip. He was pulling at her hand, which was placed firmly over his eyes. Her own eyes were wide, her face flushed.

"He didn't see anything, I made sure of that!" Alexa said breathlessly, removing her hand from the child's eyes. Dylan made an attempt to bite her fingers, which she foiled with remarkable dexterity. "But I saw plenty! Carrie, we've got to get out of here! In fact, you've got to get out of this neighborhood as soon as possible. Because if those are your neighbors in there, they're—"

"The people you saw inside aren't our neighbors," Tyler cut in flatly. He vaguely recalled that the purpose of inviting Carrie Wilcox to this party was to shock her, enabling him to buy her property when she fled the neighborhood. Therefore, shouldn't he encourage the notion that the neighbors were debauched? "None of the neighbors showed up, except you," he heard himself add.

"I caught him!" Ben's voice rang out. They all turned to see Ben jogging around the side of the house, holding Franklin under his arm like a sack, one of his hands placed firmly over the little boy's eyes, almost covering the child's entire face. He did not remove his hand until he reached the group. "Franklin didn't see a thing, Carrie, I swear."

Still gripping the restlessly twisting Emily, Carrie turned to Tyler. "Why did you invite us to this party?" she asked quietly.

Tyler felt a dull flush spread from his neck to his face. Her cool calm unnerved him far more than any angry condemnation or accusation she might have flung at him. Her blue eyes were clear and unwavering, her expression . . . was unreadable.

And that bothered him greatly because he excelled at reading people, at understanding their reactions, examining their motives, anticipating their wants and needs. It was an invaluable talent, one he used skillfully and successfully time after time in the competitive, often cutthroat world of business.

He used his gifts well in personal situations, as well. He could glance at Alexa, know that she was shocked, and decide exactly what to say to her; one look at Ben showed that he was intrigued, which required a wholly different set of responses.

But he couldn't read Carrie Wilcox. Her eyes, her face, her voice and body language gave nothing away. He didn't know if she was shocked or angry or hurt or frightened; he didn't know if she found the entire debacle amusing and was secretly laughing at him.

It had always been a point of pride with him never to be the first to break a gaze. But this time Tyler averted his eyes from Carrie's deep blue ones, losing his first-ever round in what he called "the eye contact sincerity game." His mouth was dry and his pulse beat unpleasantly fast. He was totally disconcerted.

What on earth was happening to him? He'd been leveled by this young woman. Had this been a tense business negotiation, he'd have lost it! The competition had better never find and hire Carrie Wilcox!

"It doesn't matter, anyway. We're leaving now," Carrie said in those same measured tones. The fact that he hadn't answered her question didn't seem to have fazed her. She remained completely unreadable and unreachable.

And that, Tyler realized in a sudden flash of insight, was what really confounded him. He was skilled and smooth and so adept with words and style, the Great Communicator had nothing on him, but Carrie Wilcox was beyond his reach.

After all, what good were words and charm when she rendered him mute with that steady blue-eyed gaze of hers?

Carrie put Emily into the wagon, and Alexa and Ben immediately followed suit, setting Dylan and Franklin in behind their sister. Tyler watched Carrie pull the wagon away and onto the sidewalk. She turned to say something to the small triplets, and the three of them began to wave their hands and boisterously shout, "Bye-bye-bye-bye." Carrie herself said nothing, nor did she glance his way.

"You should be ashamed of yourself, Mr. Tremaine," Alexa said indignantly as she stalked out the gate after them. "I mean, who cares what you and your sleazy friends do, but inviting my sister and the babies here was unconscionable."

Her shock had turned to anger—Tyler clearly perceived that. He knew how to deal with it, if he should care to. Right now, he didn't.

"You have to understand, Tyler, my sisters aren't at all—uh—worldly," Ben interjected.

"And you are?" Tyler asked dryly. Ben's interest was piqued; he appeared torn between leaving with his family and joining the party. Tyler perceived all of that, too. And knew how to deal with it, of course. But it was of little comfort that he could deal with two out of the three Shaw triplets when Carrie remained the elusive third.

"Oh yes, you see, I've lived all over the world," boasted Ben. "Our dad is a career air force officer. He and Mom are currently stationed in Germany again. I've lived in Germany, too, and in Turkey and England and six different states," he added proudly.

"I assume your sisters also shared this cosmopolitan lifestyle as well?"

"Well, yes. But they didn't get out and around as much as I did," Ben said quickly. "Girls are more sheltered, you know. Umm, at least in our family they were." He cast a quick glance toward the back of the house, where the swimming pool and cabana were located.

Tyler could guess what he'd seen there. He thought of the baby running back there and flinched.

"Benjamin Shaw, are you coming?" Alexa hollered from the sidewalk. Her tone implied that he'd better or she would do something about it.

Ben sighed. "I guess I'd better go help with the babies. Uh, thanks for inviting me to the party, Tyler."

"You sound as if you really mean that."

"I do! I'd like to—er—broaden my social life. But this— scene isn't for my sisters," Ben added earnestly.

"Well, feel free to come back to the party and—broaden your social life, after you've helped your sisters with the triplets," said Tyler. He started toward the oversize garage where his cars were housed.

"You're leaving?" Ben called after him, confused. "You're leaving your own party?"

"My social life is sufficiently broad," Tyler replied. And all he wanted right now was to be away from it.

He backed his navy blue '64 Mustang out of the driveway and into the street while Alexa and Ben Shaw stood on the sidewalk, staring after him. Carrie and her children were already in their front yard, and he saw a flash of red, white, blue and blond clambering out of the wagon as he drove past them.

He watched them in the rearview mirror until he turned a corner and they disappeared from his sight.

Three

Carrie sat on the two-seater aluminum glider on her small screened-in back porch. Though it was past 2:00 a.m., the party next door was still in full swing, the noise level so loud that it was as if the live band, alternating with the DJ and his collection of music discs, was right here on the porch with her. She heard voices and yells, shouts of laughter and much splashing in the pool. The scrawny hedge with its wide gap in the center was a pitifully useless sound barrier.

She sipped her iced tea, wondering how the babies could sleep through this racket, and grateful that they were. She'd turned the room air conditioner in the nursery on low, so perhaps its humming noise was masking the thunderous drums and caterwauling from the guests next door. Ben and Alexa had already left, Alexa apologetically at ten because the noise was giving her a headache, Ben an hour earlier, no excuse offered.

Sleuth, the adopted tomcat, snoozed on the big, fan-backed chair opposite her, oblivious to the tumultuous revelry next door.

Carrie sighed, wishing she could ignore it all, too, longing for the sweet oblivion of sleep, but she realized the impossibility of that. She was wide-awake, alone and annoyed, while next door...

She gave the glider a swing and thought about what Alexa and Ben had told her they'd seen during their brief foray into what Tyler Tremaine had casually labeled a "picnic." Some picnic! An awed and impressed Ben had described it quite differently—"the embodiment of every fantasy!" he'd proclaimed.

"Not any of my fantasies!" Alexa had countered crossly. "Or yours, either, Carrie."

"The only fantasy I have is getting eight uninterrupted hours of sleep," Carrie had replied. She felt about a hundred years old. Now, hours after that conversation with her siblings, she felt even older, a weary 110.

At first she wasn't sure that she'd heard the rustling in the branches of the hedge, not with so many other noises dominating the sound waves. But her eyes provided indisputable evidence to her beleaguered ears. Outlined by the floodlights next door was the silhouette of a man pushing through the branches, breaking them as he tried to make his way through the hedge. Carrie knew it was a measure of his drunkenness that he didn't use the clearly visible and convenient gap in the hedge but tried instead to go through its thickest part.

Sleuth's ears perked, his well-conditioned self-preservatory instincts suddenly on alert. He jumped down from the chair and bolted into the house through the kitchen door which stood slightly ajar. Carrie grimaced. That's what happens when you adopt a cat instead of a German shepherd, she thought wryly. She would have to face the intruder all on her own.

However, there was no way for the intruder to know that she didn't have a killer guard dog crouched by her side. She stood up and walked to the door of the porch, just as the man, tall and disheveled, tumbled through the hedge into her backyard.

"Get out of here!" Carrie called sharply. "I have a dog who's been trained to attack when I give the word. And if you don't leave right now, I'll say it."

"Gotta go," the man mumbled drunkenly, stumbling toward the porch. He looked to be in his late twenties or early thirties and was well-dressed, though his expensive clothes were showing definite strains of a night of hard partying.

"Yes, you have to go!" Carrie reiterated sternly. "You have to get out of here right now or you'll be dog meat, mister. Down, Demon! Heel, boy," she added, for effect.

"Gotta go," the young man muttered, and from his actions, Carrie suddenly realized they were each using different meanings of the word. Her eyes widened when he fumbled with the zipper of his fly as he headed straight for her flower bed.

"Not there!" she snapped, her fear turning to anger. "You'll kill my impatiens. If you must, at least use the back corner of the yard. Nothing's living over there." Sleuth had already appropriated that dead zone as his own.

Her uninvited guest stood slack-jawed and mute, looking stupidly confused.

"Oh, for heaven's sakes!" Carrie exploded. "Turn around." The man obeyed. "Now walk straight ahead, to the back corner of the yard. That's right, keep walking." She watched as he followed her orders, feeling inordinately disgusted. Not only was this jerk using her yard as his bathroom, she had to provide him with directions. What a truly hellish night this was!

She sank back down onto the glider, waiting for the drunken idiot to finish so she could direct him back to the

Tremaine "picnic." And then she heard the branches of the hedge rustle again and she jumped to her feet, enraged.

"No!" she called furiously. "Not again. Absolutely no one else can come over. I won't have my yard used as the neighborhood outhouse! Why don't you just—just use your host's pool?"

"What an uncharitable suggestion!" Tyler Tremaine was striding toward the porch, looking crisp and unrumpled, his designer polo shirt and well-fitting khaki slacks as neatly pressed as when she'd seen him hours earlier. Unlike his guest, he appeared virtually untouched by all that hearty partying. "Fortunately, I make it a practice to have the pool drained and cleaned after every party."

"From what I've heard about the goings-on in that pool, you should have it permanently sealed with a slab of concrete," Carrie retorted. She stood behind the closed screen door, her arms folded in front of her chest, and glowered balefully at Tyler, who stopped on the other side.

"You look like a disapproving schoolmarm," he observed.

"Well, I feel like I'm living next to a reform school for obnoxious delinquents. One of them—Nature Boy—is over there." She pointed to the drunk standing in the far corner of the yard, his back to them. "Why don't you go see if he needs any help?"

"Not me. That's not my scene. He'll have to manage on his own."

Tyler had barely finished speaking when the other man's knees suddenly buckled. They both watched him crumple to the ground.

"Oh, great!" Carrie scowled. "You're conveniently off the hook now. Since he passed out in my yard, I suppose that makes him my responsibility." She shoved open the porch door, her action so quick and unexpected that Tyler had to jump out of the way to avoid being slammed by it.

Feeling the damp grass cool under her bare feet, she strode through the yard, despite the fact that she was clad only in pajamas. The two-piece cotton set, teal-blue boxer-like shorts and a matching oversize camp shirt, looked more like sportswear than pajamas, anyway, Carrie decided.

Tyler followed her. It did not escape his notice that she was clad only in pajamas. He rather appreciated that she didn't offer a coy apology for her attire—or the lack of it. He well knew that standard ploy drew even more attention to the aforementioned apparel. And then he frowned. Didn't she want him to notice her? And if not, why not? In his experience, women always wanted to be noticed by Tyler Tremaine.

Carrie came to a halt beside the young man's prone figure.

"What are you going to do?" Tyler asked curiously. A light breeze ruffled her loose pajama shirt, momentarily outlining the soft, swelling curves of her breasts. Tyler blinked rapidly. Were his eyes playing tricks on him or had he seen her nipples budding tautly against the teal-blue cotton cloth?

Carrie ignored his stare and his quick, sharp gulp for air. She was concentrating solely on the unconscious man lying in the grass before her. "For starters, I thought I'd see if he's still breathing."

The man gave a sudden loud snort and started to snore.

"I guess that answers your question," observed Tyler. "Now what?"

Carrie heaved an exasperated sigh. "Well, I can't just leave him out here, can I?"

"Why not? It's a warm night and it's not raining, so that rules out his demise from hypothermia or drowning. Look at it this way, he's camping out. Sleeping under the stars. Think of all those hardy campers who pay campground fees for that privilege. Lucky Ted is doing it right here for free."

Carrie threw him a quelling glance. "His name is Ted?"

"Ted Qualter. Has a cushy government job, a political appointment, courtesy of his rich daddy who refused to allow him to work in the family firm. It was a wise decision because young Ted is an incompetent bozo."

"So they put him in government instead? My hard-earned tax dollars go to pay this—this incompetent, drunken bozo's salary?"

"Appalling, isn't it?" Tyler watched her walk around to stand in front of Ted Qualter's feet. She carefully lifted one of his feet, and then the other.

Tyler's eyes slid over her. She was small, but her legs were long and smooth and shapely. And enticingly bare. Rounded thighs. Well-shaped calves, slender ankles. Tyler realized that he was mouth-breathing. He ridiculed himself for practically drooling over her—it looked as though she was wearing her brother's pajamas! In the meantime, there were plenty of women right next door wearing...

Tyler shook his head, as if to clear it. What those women were or weren't wearing could not even be compared to Carrie's decidedly unsexy getup, yet he wasn't over there lusting after any of them. He was here, gaping at Carrie Shaw Wilcox, who was scarcely aware of his presence. Except, perhaps, as an irritant.

Oblivious to Tyler's intimate scrutiny of her, Carrie tucked Ted Qualter's feet under her arms and firmly clasped his legs with her hands.

Tyler watched the contortions of her supple body as she concentrated on her task. "Carrie, what are you doing?" he asked raspily.

"Can't you tell? I'm dragging him." She gave Ted Qualter's inert body a ferocious tug, but didn't budge him an inch. Carrie tried again, then dropped his feet. "I'm trying to drag him," she amended, gasping. "He's as heavy as a ton of cement!"

"Where did you intend to drag him? Surely you're not planning to put him up in your house for the rest of the night?"

"I'll tell you exactly what I'm planning. I'm going to get him inside, call a cab to take him home and offer the cabbie extra money to tuck Ted Qualter safely into his own bed. And I'm going to charge it all to you." She determinedly picked up Qualter's feet again. "Are you going to help me? If not, please go back to your *picnic*. I'm sure your guests are missing you."

Her inflection left no doubts as to her opinion of the party. Unlike earlier in the evening, Tyler was reading her loud and clear. "No, they're not. I haven't been around all night. I left the party when you did. I'd just returned and was pulling into the driveway when I saw Qualter thrashing around the hedge, so I followed him down here."

"Why?"

"Why did I follow him? I really don't know. Curiosity? A chivalrous impulse, perhaps? Take your pick." Tyler lifted Qualter under his shoulders. "I can manage by myself—you can put his feet down."

Carrie dropped them gladly. "A chivalrous impulse?" she repeated mockingly. "You were going to protect me from him?"

"I didn't know you were out here. Maybe I thought I'd prevent him from vandalizing your property. Save myself the hefty lawsuit you'd undoubtedly file against me for being the causative agent."

"Your party being the cause that he was here in the first place. I see. Are you always so suspicious or do I strike you as exceptionally litigious?"

"A man in my position can never be too careful," Tyler said in a tone as droll as her own.

"And is a man in your position also required to perform odd tasks, to avoid the incessant threat of being sued?" She trotted alongside as Tyler dragged the other man toward the house with commendable ease. "This particular odd task being one of them."

"Dragging a body, you mean? You have to admit, I'm quite adept at it."

"Oh, you are. If I ever need to dispose of another one, you'll be the first person I'll call."

"Aha, is that a smile I see on your face? Is your unmitigated disgust beginning to fade? We're finally starting to have fun, aren't we?"

"No, to every question," she assured him. She held open the porch door, then the door to the kitchen as Tyler dragged Qualter inside.

He followed her through the house, finally laying the man down on the floor in the front hall, the very place where he had first met Carrie, just yesterday afternoon. Carrie stayed behind in the kitchen, placing the call to the taxi company.

"They said the taxi will be here in about twenty minutes," she said, joining Tyler a few minutes later. "You can leave the cab fare and go home now."

"In a hurry to get rid of me?" Tyler smiled sardonically. "Well, I'm in no hurry to leave. I can't go home. My home has been taken over by rapacious party-goers, remember? And they'll be there until they wind down and/or sleep it off, which will probably be sometime late tomorrow afternoon."

"Am I supposed to feel sorry for you? Because I don't. It's your own fault that your house is filled with those people."

"Oh, I certainly won't deny that." Tyler shrugged. "It's my own damn fault, all right."

Carrie eyed him puzzledly. "I don't get you. You throw this big, wild party and then you leave it. You're hanging out here instead of over there with all your friends."

"And I surely do have a lot of friends, don't I?" Tyler drawled. "I wonder if half the people partying in my home tonight have ever met me? And if anyone has realized that I've been gone for the past seven hours.''

''What is this? A chorus of the poor little rich boy blues?''

''Please don't accuse me of that!'' Tyler held up one hand, grinning. ''I've never bought into that poor little rich kid crap, not even when I was a little rich boy. I've always enjoyed my status. Now that I'm a rich man, I appreciate the privileges, opportunities and luxuries that go with my fortune and position even more.''

''Well, it's refreshing to hear someone finally admit it,'' said Carrie. ''Because it seems like every time I turn on the television or pick up a magazine, some spoiled rich dope is whining about the burdens of having money. It makes me crazy! I'd like to see them try the alternative, living without it, having to worry over every cent spent, scraping and saving.''

''Is this your life you're describing?'' interrupted Tyler, frowning.

''No, not exactly. But close enough, I guess.'' Carrie looked sheepishly at the ground. ''I know I shouldn't complain—so many people are far worse off.''

''Didn't your husband leave you and the triplets well-provided for? Didn't he have a good life insurance policy?''

''Ian didn't have any life insurance. He was only twenty-five when he died, and the triplets hadn't even been born yet. Why would we need life insurance?'' Carrie's laugh was painfully ironic. ''After all, young husbands don't die. A twenty-four-year-old woman in her second month of pregnancy won't be widowed.''

''The invulnerability of youth,'' Tyler said quietly.

She smiled wistfully, and her blue eyes were sad. ''I don't suffer from that anymore.''

She looked soft and young and vulnerable. But Tyler was the one who felt weak. He looked at her, feeling inexorably drawn to her. He raised his hand, feeling an overwhelming urge to touch her, to establish some connection between them. He dropped it just as quickly. Because he wanted to touch her so much, he didn't dare allow himself to do so. A paradoxical reaction for a man who was accustomed to doing exactly as he pleased, rules be damned.

Just as abruptly, Carrie straightened, squaring her shoulders firmly, her expression mirroring her determination. "I don't indulge in fits of self-pity, either," she said defiantly. "And I certainly don't want or need *you* feeling sorry for me. I may not be in your income bracket, but I manage. I have social security survivors' benefits for the triplets and I make a decent salary."

"You work?"

"No, my fairy godmother pays the utility bills and makes the car payments. She waves her wand, and food and clothing and toys magically appear in place."

"I deserved that." Her humor touched him as much as her insistent courage. He really should get out of here, Tyler warned himself. Because if he stayed... "What sort of work do you do?" he asked, staying instead of leaving, ignoring his own wise counsel and not even caring that he'd done so. "And how do you manage a job with three babies to take care of?"

"I'm a nurse at the Hospital Center, in the labor and delivery suites. It's a wonderful place to work. So much happiness and hope and promise." Her expression was warm and bright. "It's so... *real*. Life affirming, you know?"

The cynic in Tyler surfaced. He was liking her far too much, and it was time to create some distance. "Yes, I know exactly what you mean. I could describe my chosen field of marketing in the same glowing terms."

Satisfied, he waited for her retaliation to his sarcasm. Perhaps she would throw him out, and deservedly so.

Instead, she shocked him by laughing. "Believe it or not, my brother, Ben, says the same thing about his career in advertising! He thinks a new account is more than equal to a newborn baby. Maybe even better, because a new account will produce money for the agency while a baby will cost its family money."

Tyler stared at her, feeling peculiarly as if he'd been punched in the gut. When she laughed like that, with her beautiful blue eyes glowing, her lovely mouth curved into a heart-stopping smile, he felt . . .

What? How? He could define neither these unknown feelings she was evoking within him nor the way she affected him. It was indescribable, intangible yet very real. . . . Life affirming? *So much happiness and hope and promise.* Her voice seemed to ring in his ears. Tyler sucked in his breath and tried to drag his eyes away from her. He managed to do so for at least ten seconds.

Carrie appeared unaware of his internal upheaval. She chatted on, kneeling now to check Ted Qualter's pulse. "I'm very lucky because the Hospital Center offers a schedule for nurses to work two twelve-hour shifts on weekends and get paid for a forty-hour week. I work the 7:00 p.m. to 7:00 a.m. shifts for four straight weekends and then have one off. Alexa, and sometimes Ben, stay here with the babies while I'm on duty. Not tonight, though. Needless to say, this is my free weekend."

The noise from the party next door seemed to crash and fill the silence of the darkened house. Carrie rose to her feet. "Too bad I'm not working tonight, since I'm not sleeping, anyway," she added, casting him a swift, stern glance.

Tyler cleared his throat. "I agree that the—uh—noise is intolerable."

"Of course, you were counting on that."

He looked startled. "I'm not sure what you mean by that."

"Oh, come on, Tyler, why not be honest with me? I know why you had this party and why you invited me to it."

"Do you?"

She nodded. "You wanted me to have a taste of how terrible it can be, living next door to you. How noisy and shocking and downright unwholesome for my innocent little children."

"And why would I want to do that?" Tyler asked, curious to hear her answer, in spite of himself. He realized then and there that he had underestimated her and wondered just how badly.

"You want me to sell this property to you," Carrie said frankly.

Tyler's eyes widened. Very badly, it seemed. She was right on target. Was his scheme that transparent? Or was she perceptively gifted? Whatever, she'd bested him once again.

While his thoughts bounced around his head like Ping-Pong balls, Carrie continued blithely, "You hate having this decrepit old house right next door and you probably have some big plans to build something on this lot. A tennis court, maybe? A stable for polo ponies? Or maybe a grotto and a waterfall and water slide and bigger pool for all those aquatic adventures you and your friends so enjoy."

Tyler winced. "I don't play polo and I have no intention of installing a grotto or any other—uh—water sports facility."

"Ah, the tennis court, then." She smiled at his look of consternation. "I'm right, aren't I? And you're stunned that I figured it out." She tilted her head and gazed at him squarely. "Give me some credit, Tyler. I may not be rich, but I'm not stupid."

"No, you're not. You're very bright." His voice was hoarse. "Beautiful and bright, sexy and feisty. Honest and hardworking." He gulped. "And the mother of eighteen-month-old triplets."

"You look petrified." Carrie actually laughed. "Well, you needn't be, Mr. Tremaine. I have no intention of seducing you, so you needn't worry about falling victim to my feminine wiles. You're safe from me."

Tyler stared at her, torn between wanting to join her laughter, which was unmistakably mocking, and wanting to throttle her. There was still another action he wanted to take, an alternative that seemed irresistible, given the intense interest she aroused in him.

"Maybe you're the one who should be worried." His eyes held a predatory gleam. "Suppose I decide to seduce *you* and you fall victim to my masculine charms? I've been told they're...considerable." He took a step closer to her, then another.

"I'm sure they are." Carrie stood her ground, not backing up even an inch, though he now was standing so close that his body brushed hers. "Regardless, I'm immune."

"Are you?" The soft feel of her body under her cotton pajamas brushing against him sent a jolt of sensual electricity through him. He stared down into her face, mesmerized by it. "Let's see."

"Hmm, the obligatory pass, I presume?"

"I'm going to kiss you, Carrie. I want to, and you want me to."

"Not only the obligatory pass, but it's complete with the routine stock phrases."

Tyler smiled, against his will. "If you're trying to make me laugh—"

"I'm trying to dampen your ardor by deflecting you with humor," Carrie amended. "Is it working?"

"Not when you're wriggling against me like that."

"Oops, sorry. I'll stay still as a stone. Well, go on then, complete your pass. I've resigned myself to it. I'll let you kiss me once and save you the trouble of chasing me around the room for it." Carrie grinned cheekily at him.

Tyler gazed down into the humorous warmth of her eyes, and his breath caught in his throat. For the first time in a long, long time, he found himself intrigued and excited by the mere prospect of a kiss. "I think I'll take you up on your generous offer."

Carrie felt the hard strength of his hands on her shoulders, felt the warmth of his body heat penetrating into her. With a sort of detached calm, she watched his head descend toward her, her eyes taking in every detail of his face. His sharp blade of a nose, his unique green eyes, now half-closed, his jaw shadowed and virile, in need of a shave at this late hour. And then there was his compellingly sensual mouth, his lower lip, full and well-shaped. Enticed and fascinated, she focused on it. Suddenly, she was neither detached nor calm.

A keen rush of sexual awareness surged through her. Startled, Carrie placed her hands on his chest, intending to push him away.

Instead, Tyler covered her hands with his, and rested his forehead against hers. "Scared?"

"No, it's worse than that," she whispered. His thumbs had slipped under her hands and were caressing her palms; his warm breath mingled with hers. Carrie fought the urge to close her eyes and give in to the sensuality of the moment. "I wish I were scared."

"Now, why would you wish that?" He was enjoying this game, the teasing, the push-pull sexual play that would inevitably lead right where he intended it to. He slid his hands over her, delighting in the feel of her, small and feminine yet strong and supple.

Carrie stared at his temptingly sexy mouth, and a sensual shiver rippled up her spine. Somehow, as if of their own volition, her arms raised and her hands locked at the nape of his neck. She stood on tiptoe, pressed tightly against him, inhaling his heady male scent and relishing the hard, unyielding masculine planes of his body. It had been so long since she'd been held, so long since she'd felt the ardent pulsing of a man's body, wanting her.

"You're making me feel things I thought I'd never feel again, and that's far more dangerous than being afraid of you," she said softly.

He slipped one powerful thigh between hers, interlocking her even more closely to him. "So you're not so immune to me, after all?" he teased, nibbling on the delicate softness of her earlobe.

"I guess not." She gazed up at him, her blue eyes round with surprise. She'd thought these feelings rioting through her had been buried with Ian. But to have them resurrected by a man like Tyler Tremaine, a man whose financial and social status—not to mention his level of experience—were aeons removed from her own, was disturbing indeed.

She frowned. "Now your already overinflated ego will swell even more."

Tyler laughed huskily. "It's not my ego that's swelling, honey." Easing her back against the wall, he gripped her firmly, and slowly, deliberately raised his knee until she was practically astride his muscled thigh.

Carrie clutched at him, shocked by the intimate contact, dazed by the fiery intensity burning within her. A dangerous excitement pounded through her and she wanted to flee from it as much as she wanted to stay and experience it.

And then his mouth was on hers and she couldn't think at all; she couldn't worry or reason or analyze because her thought processes seemed to have shut down, overpowered by the purely physical need rushing through her.

She parted her lips for the surge of his tongue, whimpering slightly at the excruciatingly sensual penetration. Aroused and emotional, Carrie kissed him back, holding nothing in reserve. Her hands smoothed over him as pleasure exploded her senses. Intoxicated by his taste and touch, she wanted more and more of him.

He hadn't expected her response to be so passionate, both hungry and giving. Tyler's mind reeled in a daze of erotic sensations. Once again, he had underestimated her. He'd never dreamed that he could be so roused, so rocked by one kiss. God, could she kiss! Who'd have dreamed that sweet, spunky little Carrie—the wholesome mother of three—could incite his passion so quickly, so hotly?

A sharp, urgent need shook Tyler to his very core. The sensations surging through him were raw and wild, stronger than anything he had ever known. He'd certainly experienced the heights of desire but what he was feeling now was a higher high, drawing him in, rendering him powerless to its force.

"Carrie..." He groaned her name as his mouth sought the slender curve of her neck. He was so hard he had to grit his teeth against the pleasurable pain. Groaning, he clutched her tighter as his mouth sought hers again.

And then it was all over, and he was standing alone. Carrie had wrenched herself out of his arms and stood facing him across the vestibule, the length of the supine Ted Qualter between them. It was only a small distance, but she was safely out of his reach. Tyler felt frustration tear through him. It required an alarming amount of willpower not to step over Qualter and pull Carrie back into his arms.

"That wasn't such a good idea," she said, staring at the floor.

"What?" Dazed and bemused, Tyler gazed at her, as if transfixed. His emotions were dangerously and uncharacteristically close to the surface, and the urge to give in to them, to act upon them, was tempting indeed.

"That kiss," Carrie said baldly, meeting his eyes. "It was a mistake, for both of us."

"You liked it," Tyler countered, stung. "In fact, you loved it. You were with me all the way, baby, and don't try to say that you weren't."

"I won't. But you and I have no business kissing each other. We're both adults, Tyler, and we both know where that kiss was headed."

Her frankness caught him off guard. "To the bedroom," he said bluntly, realizing that he'd failed to supply the smooth, unctuous reply that could have allowed him to take control of the conversation. And of the situation. He felt confused and off balance.

Carrie appeared just the opposite. "Yes," she said. "And that must not be allowed to happen, Tyler. We can't be lovers—we can't even be friends. You know it as well as I do." She sounded calm and decisive, in full control of the conversation, of the situation. And of him.

"No, I don't know that." Tyler didn't like it, not at all. *He* was the leader, the one who guided conversations and situations in the direction of his choice. Unfortunately, he had no idea where he wanted to go with this. "But I'm sure you're going to explain it all to me, aren't you?"

"If you'd like," Carrie said patiently.

Tyler felt patronized; he couldn't remember the last time he'd been condescended to—perhaps never. And she didn't even seem aware that she'd insulted him. She was certainly a domineering type, he decided, glaring at her. Used to giving orders and directions to those overwrought women about to deliver in the birthing suite where she worked, used to exercising complete control over her children. She obviously extended her controlling ways to anyone who happened to cross her path—or who kissed her.

"I'm a widow with three children and you're probably one of the most eligible bachelors in the city...who knows, maybe in the whole country. We're from two different worlds, that's for sure, and it's simply a geographical quirk of fate that we ever happened to meet at all."

Tyler sighed impatiently. "This is getting tedious. Kindly make your point."

"My point is this—I don't have the time or energy or interest to get sexually involved with anyone." Carrie shrugged. "And from what I've gleaned about your lifestyle, you certainly don't have the time or energy or interest to be nonsexually involved, especially with someone like me."

"Is that so?"

She nodded, her expression serious, her blue eyes intense. She sincerely believed everything she was saying. Tyler was hit once again with a barrage of conflicting urges. He wanted to laugh at her earnestness, he wanted to argue those stupid, dogmatic points of hers, and most of all, he wanted to drag her back into his arms and kiss her senseless.

While he was mulling his options, Carrie spoke up. "There's one more thing."

He grimaced wryly. "I can't wait to hear it."

She took a deep breath and forged ahead. "Maybe, hopefully, I'm wrong, but if you're planning to romance me into selling this house to you, please don't waste your time."

"I hadn't planned on doing anything of the kind!" Tyler snapped. "What kind of a man do you think I am?"

"A very rich one who is used to getting his own way and having what he wants."

"That was a rhetorical question. You didn't have to answer it," he grumbled.

Carrie ignored the interruption. "You will have this property, Tyler," she continued earnestly. "I promise to sell to you eventually, but I don't want to move the children again just yet. We've moved four times since they were born, and I'd like them to have a sense of familiarity with one place for a while before we move again. I'd also like to avoid moving again with three babies." She smiled wearily. "You can't imagine how difficult that is. When they're about three, I'll brave it again. That isn't too long for you to wait, is it? Only about eighteen months and then we can negotiate a sale and—"

"I do not care to discuss a real estate transaction at this point in time," Tyler exclaimed, exasperated. He wanted her so badly he was aching from his head to his heels with the force of it, and she was utterly dispassionate, controlled and impervious to him. While he was hungering for the taste of her luscious pink mouth, she seemed bent on discussing the sale of her property to him at some future date.

He remembered very well that his goal had been to purchase the property, using whatever means necessary to get her to agree to sell. Why and how had that goal suddenly been rendered...irrelevant? Tyler was thunderstruck by the insight. Whatever was occurring now, the property was definitely not a factor. *What was going on here, anyway?*

"I think I hear the taxi," Carrie said, hurrying to the door.

Tyler watched her go, wondering how anyone could hear anything with the racket going full blast next door. He could hardly hear himself think; perhaps that was the reason his thoughts, usually keen, precise and penetrating, right now were anything but. It was as if he were drunk, but he'd had nothing stronger than the bottled water he kept in the refrigerator in his office, where he'd spent the past seven hours working.

He was disconcerted, disturbed. Nothing was as it should be. Women did not muddle his thoughts; they stayed in the recreation-and-diversion compartment of his mind until he felt like thinking about them. Carrie had not only broken out of the compartment, she had invaded and disrupted his thought processes much as a technological virus infects the workings of a computer. He needed an antidote and fast!

Carrie reentered the house with the taxi driver in tow. The man was short and wiry and did not look pleased at the prospect of hauling off the snoring, immobile Ted Qualter. "Lady, this is going to cost you plenty," he muttered.

Tyler was relieved to stop thinking. It was time to take action. "Don't worry, it'll be worth your while," he promised the driver.

The two men hoisted Qualter to his feet and half carried, half dragged him out of the house. Carrie watched from the doorway as they dumped the limp body into the back seat of the cab. She saw Tyler withdraw a money clip from his pocket and offer some bills to the cabbie who departed the scene with a wide grin.

Tyler walked back to her. "You made the driver a happy man," she said.

"Yes. He's been very well paid for his efforts." Tyler shrugged. "As you so astutely pointed out earlier, I am a rich man who is used to getting his own way and having what he wants. I wanted Qualter gone from the premises."

"Thank you," Carrie said gravely. "I would've hated to have him lying here on the floor when the kids woke up." She glanced at her watch. "Which they'll be doing in about four hours. I have to try to get some sleep."

"So do I, but it'll be impossible with those morons carrying on at my house. Mind if I stay here?"

"You're kidding, right?"

"Wrong. If you don't have an extra bedroom, I'll just use the sofa in the living room."

"Tyler—"

"I promise not to try to ravage you. I won't even touch you. You see, I agree that we can't be lovers, but I do think we can be friends."

He was confident and in control again; he felt exultant. The solution had come to him as he'd loaded Qualter into the cab. Friendship! Tame, boring and uneventful friendship. *That* was the antidote to this unexpected, unnerving spell she seemed to have cast over him, the cure to this absurd interest he'd developed in her. Frequent doses of her company would naturally dilute her appeal; it was inevitable. Especially without sex as an incentive. Tyler smiled, well pleased with his strategy.

Carrie folded her arms and stared directly into his glittering green eyes. "Why would you want to be friends with me?"

"Why wouldn't I want to?" he countered smoothly. "After all, we are neighbors. It's perfectly natural and reasonable for neighbors to be friendly."

Carrie sighed. "Then I'm asking, friend to friend, will you please leave? You can't stay, and I'm too tired to stand here arguing with you about it."

"You really want me to leave? You'd send me over to that den of iniquity, filled with wanton women only too eager to have their wicked way with me? What kind of a friend are you, Carrie?"

His tone was light and Carrie knew he was joking, although she had no doubts about the veracity of his claim. All those women . . . She felt an odd little pang deep within her, and entirely unbidden came the torrid memory of that hot, hot kiss they had shared.

Carrie stole a quick, furtive glance at him and found him watching her, his green eyes intent. She wondered if he knew what she was thinking and decided that he probably did, that he'd said what he'd said to evoke that very memory. He was experienced, sophisticated and calculating, and it was time to send him on his way. Immediately.

"I have a can of Mace I'll be glad to lend you, if you really want to fend off all those amorous attacks," she said lightly.

"Carrie—"

"Goodbye and good night, Mr. Tremaine."

"What, no more Tyler? After all we've shared?" He laughed. "Lighten up, Carrie. Loosen up. We like each other and there's no reason why we can't be friends."

"Why are you suddenly so insistent on being friends with me?" she demanded.

Tyler stared thoughtfully at the ground. She wanted an answer but the truth wouldn't quite serve. This was where his years of marketing strategies and counterstrategies served him well.

"Maybe it's because you said we can't be friends in that doomsday tone of yours," he said ingenuously. "I don't like to be told what I can and can't do. In fact, I don't like the concept of *can't* at all. As soon as someone tells me something can't be done, I set about trying to see that it can. So how about it, Carrie?" He offered her his hand. "Friends?"

"Oh, well, why not?" Carrie put her hand in his, and they shook like two business partners agreeing on a verbal contract. "All things considered, I guess I'd rather have you as a friend than an enemy. And since we're friends, we can be honest and open with each other, right?"

"I doubt if you could be anything but," he murmured. He had the strongest urge to lift her hand to his mouth and press his lips against her small, warm palm. He pictured her gazing at him, dazed and charmed.

"Okay, here goes." Carrie withdrew her hand from his and flashed him a dazzling smile. "Tyler, old pal, it's time for you to get lost. And I mean that in the most friendly, honest, and open way."

Four

Tyler heard baby voices and squeals of laughter and the sound of splashing water as he approached the gap in the hedge separating his property from Carrie's. He hesitated, glancing back at his house, which stood cool and quiet under the hot noon sun. Most of the party guests were gone, though a few still slept on in various rooms, sprawled on furniture or the floor, and about five or six were currently preparing some sort of breakfast for themselves in the enormous, tiled kitchen. Tyler had listened to their post-party ramblings for a few minutes and been seized by an inexplicable urge to escape.

He'd immediately fled the scene and now here he was, wearing cutoff jeans and nothing else, staring at the trail-beaten gap in the unsightly hedge. From the sounds of it, Carrie's children were playing in the backyard. Tyler frowned, realizing at that moment how much he'd been hoping for a replay of last night. That he would find her alone in her yard and they would . . .

They would what? he asked himself cynically. Pick up where they'd left off last night? And where would that be? The part where he had kissed her and they'd both burned with unslaked desire, or the part where she'd told him to get lost, gave him a friendly shove out the door and locked it behind him?

It felt odd, wondering about a woman. He viewed the opposite sex as an open book, one he had no trouble reading. His preoccupation with Carrie might have alarmed him if he hadn't already developed a workable course of action for dealing with it. Tyler congratulated himself on his foresight. It was so simple, so basic. The more he saw of Carrie, the less interest she would hold for him. Any marketing student with an elementary grasp of the dangers of overexposure was familiar with that theory. More is less. And Tyler Tremaine had an advanced degree in marketing.

His plan, however, did not include exposure to Carrie's three little kiddies, especially not on the minimal amount of sleep he'd gotten last night. Tyler turned to head back up to the house.

"Dylan, come back! No, no, Dylan. Don't go over there!"

Carrie's voice stopped Tyler in his tracks. A moment later he heard a shriek of victory as a small blond tyke, clad in a boxy pair of green swim trunks printed with yellow ducks, came barreling through the gap in the hedge.

With a sense of inevitability, Tyler swooped down and caught the fugitive, swinging him up in his arms.

"Go!" Dylan demanded, struggling and wriggling impatiently.

"You mean 'go home,'" Tyler amended as he carried the toddler back through the hedge.

Dylan stopped moving and looked at him curiously. "Go ho?"

"Happy to oblige you. Home you go," Tyler assured him. "And I sincerely hope you'll stay there." He squinted against the sun to see Carrie running toward them, clutching a child on each hip.

"Looks like both your arms are fully occupied," Tyler noted drolly. "How did you plan to catch this one—with your teeth?" He shook his head. "The logistics of toddler triplets are mind-boggling, especially in your case. It's three against one."

He wasn't telling her anything she didn't already know. Carrie shrugged. "I couldn't leave Emily and Franklin alone in the pool." She was breathless from the heat and exertion. "They could slip under the water within seconds. Better that I try to catch Dylan with my teeth."

Tyler smiled. He liked her can-do spirit. None of that poor-helpless-little-me whining for her. She probably *could've* caught Dylan with her teeth!

He looked over her shoulder and saw the round blue plastic pool, half-filled with water, standing across the yard. Then he glanced down at Carrie, who was wearing a modestly cut two-piece swimsuit, bright yellow with white polka dots. Her legs were quite long for someone of her petite stature, he noted, remembering he'd noticed that last night, too. And her legs were very shapely, from ankle to thigh. He found himself staring appreciatively.

"You seem to be making a habit of this," said Carrie.

Tyler jerked his eyes away, and to his consternation, a guilty flush stained his neck. "Uh, I don't know what you mean." An elementary principle—when caught in the act, stonewall!

"Catching my runaways," Carrie said, smiling up at him. "First Emily last night, then Dylan today. Thank-you once again."

Tyler swallowed hard. Her legs were definitely a weapon, but her smile and those intense blue eyes of hers were an arsenal all their own. He stared at her, bemused.

"Bath," Franklin exclaimed, pointing to the little pool. He was wearing white swim trunks printed with green frogs.

Emily wore a ruffled pink bathing suit and was doing her upside down trick, hanging over Carrie's arm.

"Bath," echoed Dylan excitedly, nearly jumping out of Tyler's arms. Tyler tightened his grip, a bit more adept at coping with the wriggling bundle than he'd been last night, with the gymnastics-prone Emily.

"Bath! Bath! Bath!" Everybody took up the cry, each louder than the other.

"Swim," corrected Carrie. "You're going to swim in your pool." She started across the yard toward the small blue pool.

Tyler automatically followed her. What else could he do? He was holding her kid, wasn't he? "Fim," Dylan said conversationally.

Tyler looked at him. "You mean, *swim?* Hey, you got it. Swim, not bath." He was rather impressed. He'd never actually credited babies with the ability to think, but this child had obviously listened to Carrie and comprehended her correction. His diction was pretty bad, though. "Swim," Tyler corrected. "*S-w,* not *f.*"

"Fim," repeated Dylan.

"Yeah, well, you're on the right track. Keep practicing." Tyler put Dylan into the pool as Carrie deposited Franklin and Emily there.

"Bath!" Franklin cried ecstatically, splashing in the water.

"Swim," Tyler corrected. "Say *swim.* Come on, kid, show your brother that you're as smart as he is."

"By all means, set up that competitive drive," Carrie said dryly. "After all, they're eighteen months old and it's never too soon to teach them all about competition in the global marketplace, hmm?"

"Brothers are natural competitors, nobody has to teach them to be," Tyler retorted. "My earliest memories are of trying to beat my older brother at any game I could—at *anything* I could." He smiled reminiscently. "Of course, since Cole was three years older, I never had any luck there, but I did have the extreme good fortune to have a younger brother, Nathaniel—''

''And you were always able to win against Nathaniel, the way Cole won against you,'' Carrie surmised.

Tyler beamed. ''That's right. Every brother should have a kid brother to triumph over. Builds character.''

''Or character disorders,'' Carrie said dampeningly. ''I want my boys to be friends, not rivals.''

''Fim!'' shouted Dylan.

''Bath!'' crowed Franklin.

Carrie and Tyler looked at each other and laughed. ''Suddenly they're dueling linguists,'' Carrie said. She sat down on the edge of the rickety chaise lounge positioned by the side of the pool.

Her knees were feeling peculiarly weak. That smile of Tyler's had actually affected her physically, leaving her wide-eyed and winded, as if she'd been socked directly in the solar plexus. In addition, there was the visual impact of his bare chest—muscular, broad and hair-roughened; his long, strong legs, and his well-worn jeans that enhanced every masculine line. Oh, he wore them well, all right. Carrie gulped. She allowed her eyes to linger on him for a moment longer, before dragging her gaze away.

Tyler Tremaine was a marvelous-looking man, and he seemed to become even more attractive with every passing glance. And he knew it, of course. Carrie knew he knew it. He had that innate confidence of one who has always been admired and prized—especially by the opposite sex. Carrie was sure that she wasn't the first woman to be rendered breathless by his smile and virile physique, but this was definitely a first for her. She'd never before simply looked at a man and felt the sharp slash of sheer desire.

Carrie felt a swift stab of disloyalty toward Ian's memory. Ian had been blond and handsome and his wholesome boy-next-door looks had appealed to her from the first time she'd seen him, in the lunch line at their dormitory cafeteria six years ago. Her heart clenched, remembering that innocent time. It seemed so poignant and so sad to look back, knowing the tragic end that awaited laughing, warmhearted Ian.

Carrie slid her sunglasses, which were resting on the top of her head, down over her eyes and thought how much she loved Ian. How much she would always love him, forever and ever. Nobody would ever take his place. And if she were to occasionally glance at another man, it didn't mean a thing. She was human, wasn't she? One would have to be an android not to react, even slightly, to Tyler Tremaine's traffic-stopping looks.

Tyler stole a quick glance at Carrie. He was glad she'd put on her sunglasses; those gorgeous eyes of hers disarmed him too thoroughly. Maybe it was the intensity of the color that mesmerized him or the alert intelligence reflected in them, which made him listen more intently to her, no matter how inane the topic. Whatever, he turned his attention to the children, with something akin to relief.

"Okay, Emily, you must have an opinion on this matter." Tyler knelt beside the pool where Emily sat methodically filling a milk carton with water and emptying it into a plastic pail that floated nearby. "Let's hear the feminine viewpoint. Is this activity a bath or a swim?"

Emily gave him a long look. "Wa-ner," she said calmly, resuming her project.

"She said water," Tyler said eagerly, ignoring the mispronunciation. Carrie nodded her confirmation.

"Wow, she's the smartest one of all." Tyler was astonished. "She's made the leap that it's all water, be it a bath or a swim."

"Isn't it lucky you didn't have a sister," mocked Carrie. "She would've taken on you and your brothers and won every time."

Tyler rolled his eyes. "Your poor brother has my heart-felt sympathy. You and your sister probably led him around by the nose. From the little I've seen of the three of you to-gether, you still do."

"Don't ever let Ben hear you say that." Carrie grinned. "He's always harbored under the delusion that he is the undisputed leader of us three."

Tyler shook his head. "Poor chump."

At that moment, Franklin and Dylan each reached for the fat rubber duck floating in the middle of the pool. Franklin grabbed it by the tail just as Dylan grabbed the head.

"Mine!" Both screamed in unison.

"That's their new word," said Carrie wryly. "They learned it last week and have been using it enthusiastically ever since."

Neither child would cede the duck, and the shrieks of "Mine!" resounded through Tyler's head like gunshots. "Aren't you going to do anything?" he demanded. "They're getting awfully noisy."

"This from the man whose party blasted the entire neighborhood at nine-million-trillion decibels?" Carrie shrugged. "Anyway, they're just enjoying a little brotherly tiff. I thought you'd approve. Doesn't it bring back fond memories?"

"Well, if you can't be bothered to intervene..." Scowl-ing his disapproval, Tyler snatched the duck away from both boys and handed it to Emily who was calmly pouring and emptying, ignoring the spat entirely. "Your sister gets to keep the duck, guys," he said righteously. "You see what happens when you yell and—"

He didn't have a chance to finish. Dylan and Franklin both burst into howls of rage, crying and wailing at the top of their lungs. They advanced on Emily like a charging army. Emily took one look at the duck in her hand and an-other at her brothers and threw the toy out of the pool. It was too much for Dylan and Franklin to deal with. They began to cry in earnest, sinking down onto the floor of the pool, looking very frustrated and very, very small.

"I feel like the school bully," Tyler muttered grimly. He retrieved the duck and offered it to the boys, but both were crying too hard and refused to accept it. When he handed it to Emily, she threw it out of the pool again.

Carrie got into the pool and took Dylan and Franklin on her lap.

"How do you stand it?" Tyler stared at them, his expression a mixture of horror and awe. She had to live like this, amidst cries and babbling, twenty-four hours a day, three-hundred-sixty-five days a year. Three-sixty-six during leap year. Why, working weekends at the hospital dealing with hysterical women in labor and their panicky husbands probably felt like a vacation to her!

Carrie ignored his question, ignored him, and devoted her full attention to her sons. It took only a few moments of her cuddling and soft voice to calm the two children. Their good humor restored, they each clutched toy boats she'd handed them and crawled around the water, pushing them. Carrie got out of the water and resumed her seat on the chaise.

Neither realized that Tyler had moved closer to it, and when she sat down her leg brushed against his back. Both moved apart so quickly, it would've been humorous, if either felt like laughing. But neither did. Carrie felt as if her skin were on fire. Every nerve ending that had contacted with Tyler's muscular back tingled and burned.

Tyler still felt the silky smooth softness of her leg against him, as if she'd left a permanent, sensual imprint. He felt his body tighten, felt the pleasurable hardening rise of desire and stifled a groan. Now was definitely the time for one of the triplets to dump a bucket of cold water in his lap, or for all three of them to begin screeching again, an equally effective turnoff.

But the triplets played contentedly in the pool. Carrie and Tyler remained silent and tense with sexual awareness.

Tyler glanced covertly from Carrie to the children. They looked adorable, and watching the three of them interact was far more interesting than he could bring himself to admit. As for Carrie, she was sexy and sweet and utterly unattainable—not that he wanted to attain her, of course, but even if he had wanted to, he couldn't because he would not, could not, become involved with a mother of three. It was unthinkable.

Tyler felt a sharp, sudden wave of anger crash through him. He didn't know why but suddenly he was as infuriated as he'd been on the day that an idiot subordinate within the Tremaine Books division had mistakenly sent fifty thousand copies of *The Alternative to Beef Cookbook* to the Kansas City Cattlemen's Association.

"So this is what you do all day, huh?" He broke the silence, the sneer in his voice matching the sneer on his face. "You mediate fights among the munchkins, you chase them around, outside during warm weather, inside during cold. You feed them, you change diapers, then you feed them again so you have to change diapers again. Day in and day out, repetitious, tedious and unending, with never a moment to yourself. Pretty hellish existence, if you ask me."

"Who asked you?" Carrie snapped, then answered her own question. "Nobody did. And nobody asked you to come over and stay either. If you find it so hellish to be around us, then get out of here!"

Tyler looked at her. She had whipped off her sunglasses and was glaring at him, her blue eyes fierce and piercing, her expression one of pure fury. She was mad, boiling mad, and he shifted uncomfortably on the ground. He couldn't remember anyone ever looking at him with such pure, unabashed anger. Certainly no woman ever had.

The shock of it abruptly doused his own ire. "Don't tell me you're kicking me out again?" he attempted flippantly, flashing his most charming bad-boy grin.

Carrie was not charmed, not a bit. "Yes, I am. You're moody and you have a mean streak and I don't have to put up with any of it, not you or your bad moods or your meanness. So just—take a hike!"

"Moody? Mean? Me?" Tyler was stunned. And stung. "Your accusations are both untrue and unwarranted and incredibly insulting. I've never—"

"No, I'm sure you never have heard a few home truths about yourself," Carrie cut in hotly. "This is a first for you. You're rich and you're single and therefore, you're spoiled. Lots of women will put up with just about any kind of treatment from a rich, single guy like you because they have some stupid delusions that they might actually win you—the prince himself!—and live happily ever after with all your millions."

She paused, midtirade, to breathe. Tyler opened his mouth to speak, then closed it. What she was saying had a hideous ring of truth to it. He'd certainly been aware of his status and his appeal, and he'd certainly used both to his own advantage. His behavior hadn't always been ... exemplary. But no woman—not a single one!—had ever dared to tell him so. Until now.

"Well, I don't have to put up with you or suck up to you," Carrie ranted on. "I have nothing to lose and everything to gain by telling you to go away and don't come back."

Tyler stood and stuffed his hands into the pockets of his jeans. "You certainly have ..." His voice trailed off. He cleared his throat. *"Moxie."* It was one of his father's words, not his own, but it seemed to fit. "And while I don't look for moxie in the women I, uh, date—" he smiled sheepishly "—I find that I have to respect it in a—friend."

Carrie rose, too, and they stood, practically toe-to-toe, her glaring up at him, him gazing bemusedly down at her. "I'm not your friend," she countered.

"Last night you said you were."

"I just said it to get rid of you."

"And now you're saying you aren't, for the same alleged purpose—to get rid of me. Rather paradoxical, don't you think?"

"What I think is that you're a jerk."

Tyler grimaced. "If I leave, I won't be back, Carrie. You won't see me again."

She folded her arms, never taking her eyes from him. "Good!"

He knew she meant it, too. Tyler heaved an exasperated sigh. "So why am I still standing here? After all, I'm not nailed to the ground. Why haven't I stormed out of this wreck of a yard, thanking my good fortune for having escaped such a sharp-tongued, bad-tempered witch?"

"Except you'd spell it with a *b*," Carrie said coolly.

Tyler stared at her. She didn't look quite as angry anymore. He thought he could detect a distinct gleam of amusement beginning to glimmer in those luminous eyes of hers.

His mouth was suddenly quite dry. "Why the hell am I still here?" he asked huskily.

"I don't know. Maybe because you're awed by my moxie?"

"You're laughing at me," he said incredulously. "And you're not mad anymore." He was suddenly, unexpectedly exhilarated. And enthralled.

"I guess not." Carrie shrugged. "I admit to having the world's worst temper. I'm quick to anger but I get over it just as fast. And what you said about my life—about having to take care of the kids and all—well, it's nothing that Ben hasn't said every time he visits us. But hearing it from you..." Her voice trailed off and she shrugged again. "It offended me. I took it personally and got mad."

"So I noticed." Tyler cupped her shoulders with his hands. It felt perfectly natural to touch her. So very right. His fingers kneaded absently, feeling the delicate lines of her bones, the soft warmth of her skin. He inhaled sharply and slid his hands down the length of her arms. "Look, Carrie, I—"

She whirled away from him and stepped into the pool. "It's time for lunch," she announced brightly. "Are you hungry, kids? Hungry for lunch?" She sounded so enthusiastic that the children grew quite excited and echoed something sounding like "yunsh."

"Good! Come on," Carrie said encouragingly, helping first Emily, then Franklin, and finally Dylan out of the pool. Franklin and Dylan ran to the house. Emily paused and looked back at Tyler.

"Yunsh?" she said questioningly.

Tyler was absurdly touched. "Are you inviting me to lunch, Emily?"

Emily looked up at him with those big blue eyes of hers, looking tiny and cute with her mop of blond hair and her round, little face. She raised her small arms in an unmistakable demand to be picked up.

"You want me to carry you?" Tyler asked. Emily did not reply, but waited expectantly. Tyler scooped up the little girl and headed toward the house. He had to, he assured himself. Snubbing a one-year-old was inexcusably churlish. "Okay, I'll accept your kind invitation, Emily. I'll have lunch with you."

"Oh, no!" Carrie groaned. She opened the back porch door and the boys clambered inside. Sleuth, the cat, who had been napping on the glider, dashed into the house when he heard them coming.

"What do you mean, 'oh, no'?" demanded Tyler, trailing her into the kitchen.

"Exactly what I said. I thought you'd leave when we came inside."

"We're not fighting anymore," Tyler reminded her. "Why do you want me to leave?"

"Because you're exhausting," she said bluntly. "Being with you is exhausting. And I only had three and a half hours' sleep last night and right now I'm so tired that all I want to do is to feed the kids lunch, put them down for their naps and then crash into bed."

"I like the 'crash into bed' part." Tyler grinned wickedly. "And I am not exhausting, I'm stimulating. Ask any of the Tremaine board of directors who it is that keeps those interminable board meetings from becoming deadly boring. They'll all say it's me."

"Deadly boring can be restful. You, I repeat, are exhausting. That's why I'd like to rescind Emily's invitation to lunch."

It was true, but only the partial truth, Carrie acknowledged grimly. The full, unabridged version would have to include those tantalizing streaks of pleasure that had spun through her when he'd touched her. The almost stunning urge to melt against his big hard body, to press herself into the wiry-soft mat of hair on his chest, to rub her legs against the muscular columns of his.

She hadn't dared let it happen. She had already spent entirely too much time thinking about the way he had kissed her last night, reliving the feel and the touch and the taste of him. She'd even dreamed about it during her paltry three and a half hours of sleep.

What utter insanity! A sexual infatuation she did not need! Aside from being shamefully disloyal to poor dear Ian, getting physical with Tyler Tremaine would be sheer folly, not to mention a guarantee of misery.

The man undoubtedly was accustomed to women throwing themselves at him, to doing anything at all to please him. The only reason he was sticking around now was because she did not try to please him and he found it novel. She related to him on a wholly different level than the other women in his life because she was *not* one of the women in his life. And she fully intended to keep it that way.

"Let's take off these wet suits," she said briskly to no one in particular, reaching down to strip off Dylan's trunks. He wore a sodden diaper underneath which she removed and tossed into the trash. He took off into the hall, nude and squealing.

"Want to catch him, dry him off and put a diaper on him?" Carrie asked Tyler, who was watching her intently, little Emily still held high in his arms.

"No!"

"Well, if you insist on staying, you're going to have to make yourself useful. Would you please carry Emily and Franklin upstairs so I can change them? I'm going after Dylan."

"You asked so nicely, how can I refuse? Your wish is my command." Tyler executed a deep bow, pausing to scoop up Franklin while still hanging on to Emily.

"Monk-mey," Emily said on their way upstairs. She patted Tyler's cheek with her tiny hand. "Monk-mey."

Tyler was floored. "That's what I called you last night! Emily, you remembered!"

He told Carrie that astonishing fact as she dried off the triplets and taped fresh disposable diapers on them. "Imagine her putting that together, remembering me and the word *monkey*. Saying it to me—"

"Maybe she thinks it's your name," joked Carrie. "Or your species."

He could not be diverted by humor. "Carrie, she said it to me over twenty-four hours after I first said it to her! And I only said it one time! She is a brilliant child," he added earnestly.

"She isn't stupid," Carrie agreed, "but 'brilliant' is pushing it. Kids learn fast at this age, Tyler, and they learn new things every day." She tilted her head and gazed at him squarely. "It's exciting. It's fun. Watching the three of them learn and grow and do new things is why I don't believe that I lead—how did you put it?—a hellish existence."

"Touché," Tyler conceded. "You can give it right back," he added with grudging admiration.

"And I can dish it out, too. Keep that in mind the next time you decide to pick a fight with me."

The triplets were running around the room, flinging toys about. Tyler caught Carrie and grabbed her from behind, stopping her in her tracks. "You're a tough cookie, huh?" He was smiling, his green eyes filled with playful challenge. "A really tough broad."

"Yes." She gazed sidelong at him, her blue eyes gleaming with an age-old challenge of their own. "So don't tangle with me, mister."

"To be forewarned is to be forearmed." His arm snaked out to wrap around her midriff, pulling her back against him. "That's a battle cry we warriors in marketing chant at staff meetings." His fingers, stroking her nape, began a slow, sensuous massage.

For a moment, surprise held Carrie immobile. Then the desire she'd experienced earlier gripped her again, intensifying and overwhelming. Her eyelids snapped closed and she turned her head toward his mouth at the same moment his lips sought hers, in a mutually choreographed move so smooth it was as if they had rehearsed it together many times.

He rubbed his lips softly against her mouth, and her lips parted instantly, encouragingly, at the pressure. His hand splayed over her belly and she laid her hand over his. Their fingers interlaced at the moment their tongues touched.

There was no way he could hide the burgeoning surge of desire at her response and Tyler groaned, opening his mouth wider and harder over hers as his tongue sought an intimate erotic little duel with hers.

Carrie made a soft sound in her throat as the kiss deepened. Her breasts swelled and tightened, as if he had actually touched them. She felt a thick, syrupy warmth pool deeply in her abdomen.

Moving once again in tandem, their movements unspoken but perfectly attuned, she turned in his arms as he turned her toward him. She went on tiptoe, her arms clasped around his neck as he held her tightly pressed against him, his big hands smoothing over the supple curves of her back and buttocks, caressing, squeezing, stroking.

Their mouths impacted for a long, deep, drugging kiss that seemed to go on forever, growing hotter and wilder as they clung together in a private passionate whirlwind of intimacy and desire.

"Mama, mama!" Franklin launched himself against Carrie, fastening his small arms around her legs. "Go, go, go."

At the same time, Emily squatted down beside Tyler and, fascinated, began to pull at the wiry dark hairs on his legs. "Yikes!" he yelped painfully.

Tyler and Carrie jumped apart so swiftly that they swayed and teetered and almost fell before shakily gaining their balances.

"Yikes!" shrieked Dylan in delight. "Yikes, yikes, yikes!" He clearly loved the sound of the new word.

Tyler ran his hand through his hair. He felt dazed, unreal. Franklin's shouts of "Go" and Dylan's "Yikes" kept echoing in his head.

"Why say something once when you can say it fifty times?" he mumbled grimly. That seemed to be the triplets' motto. Automatically, he stooped to pick up Emily. "Hey, Emily, are you trying out for a position as a torturer's apprentice? That hurt!"

"Yikes," Emily said happily.

Carrie picked up Dylan and Franklin. "Time to eat," she sang out, but her voice was thick and shaky. She caught Tyler's eye and quickly looked away.

Without a word to each other, Carrie and Tyler carried the three children back to the kitchen where she tied full-size

bibs around each small neck before placing each baby in a
high chair.

Tyler sank onto a chair at the kitchen table and watched
Carrie tear ham and cheese into bite-size pieces and place it
on the three high-chair trays.

"Can I have mine in a sandwich?" he asked dryly.

Carrie tossed the packets of ham and cheese at him.
"Here's the bread, lettuce and tomatoes, too. You can make
the sandwiches while I get out the carrots and grapes." She
gave each child a few thin slices of raw carrots and some
seedless green grapes.

The triplets attacked their lunch with enthusiasm. Tyler
and Carrie watched them silently, he sitting at the table, she
standing across from it. Carrie's gaze slid covertly from the
babies to Tyler. Inadvertently, she caught him staring at her.

She quickly looked away. "You haven't even started
making our sandwiches yet," she said. Her voice was still
not as steady as she would've wished.

"I hate to cook." Tyler shoved the food away from him.

"Making two sandwiches hardly falls into the realm of
cooking." Carrie began to make the sandwiches herself,
spreading mayonnaise, then mustard, on the bread with
methodical precision.

"What's the matter?" Tyler watched her, his green eyes
intent.

"Nothing," she said quickly—too quickly, she realized.
She caught her lower lip between her teeth in a gesture of
dismay. "Why?"

"You seem—" he paused and shrugged "—different.
Edgy." He leaned forward in his chair. "Yes, very much on
edge. A bit high-strung." His eyes blazed with intensity.
"Are you thinking about—what happened upstairs?"

Five

"No, of course not!" Carrie insisted.

Tyler's eyes narrowed. "You weren't?"

She shook her head. "It was just a kiss and it—it just sort of happened." Her pulses were jumping, her heart pounding. She felt edgy and high-strung, just as Tyler had observed, but she was determined to project otherwise. "Chalk it up to basic biology. We're both adults. We can deal with it."

"That's true. It was simply chemistry. Proximity." Tyler shrugged. "It didn't mean anything. I'm glad you understand." He sounded nonchalant, even amused.

"I'm glad *you* understand," Carrie said quickly. "Because I love Ian and I'm never going to love anyone else."

Tyler nodded his understanding. "I'm glad we can be honest with each other, Carrie. I like you, and your kids are very cute, but I'll never, ever get involved with you. It's out of the question. I don't want an instant family. I've deliberately never even dated a woman with children before because I'm not interested in the surrogate daddy role, even temporarily."

"Well, I certainly don't want to date you!" Carrie was aghast. "I don't want to date anyone, ever again!"

"Not anyone? Not ever?" he asked, distracted by her vehemence. "Why not?"

"Why would I? People date when they're looking for someone to become involved with, and I'm not looking. That part of my life is over."

"There is a huge difference between dating and involvement," Tyler explained patiently. "I enjoy women's company but I don't want to get seriously involved with anyone, not at this particular point in time. Probably not for years. I told both my father and my brother so, just the other day. For what seemed like the millionth time," he added, sighing.

Carrie pushed a plate with a tall sandwich on it across the table to him. "Are they nagging you to settle down?"

"Lately it seems to be their sole topic of conversation." Tyler frowned. "I'm sick of it."

"Tell them that you don't want to get married—and be firm about it," Carrie advised. "When my family tries to gently hint that I ought to think about looking for a father to help me raise my children, I tell them in no uncertain terms that I have no intention of ever marrying again."

"Why don't you?" Tyler asked curiously. "Practically speaking, marriage could benefit you and the children, certainly in a financial sense."

"You sound like my parents." Carrie grimaced. "But realistically, what man would want to support three children who aren't his? And, anyway, you know what they say about people who marry solely for money."

"Oh, yeah, I'm real familiar with that one. Those who marry for money—"

"—earn it the hard way," Carrie chimed in.

"But finances aside, wouldn't it be easier for you if there were another adult around here?" Tyler pressed. "You're very attractive and you're very young, Carrie. There must be some guy out there who wouldn't mind marrying you, kids and all."

"But I don't want my children to be viewed as an obligatory part of a package that comes with me," Carrie said earnestly. "I want them to be valued and wanted for themselves. And what are the chances of that? I mean, you summed it up accurately and honestly when you said that you didn't want an instant family. I'm sure most men feel that way. They wouldn't mind having their own kids, but they don't want someone else's."

Tyler looked at the triplets, who were babbling to one another and grinning happily as they stuffed their lunch into their mouths with their little fingers. They were bright and cute and lovable. Even though he'd never had much interest in children, he could easily see the Wilcox triplets' appeal. It seemed sad to think that no man could want them; in fact, it was downright depressing. So typically, pragmatically, he decided to think something else.

"You know, I believe that there is some great guy out there who would be delighted to raise your kids as his own. In fact, I'm sure there is," Tyler insisted fervently.

"There already was a great guy," Carrie corrected. "His name was Ian Wilcox and he was killed two years ago when a teenage drunk in a pickup truck ran a red light and hit his car head-on."

"Ian was killed in a car accident?" Tyler was taken aback. He stood up and began to restlessly pace the floor. "That's how my mother died. Her car was hit from behind while she was stopped to make a left turn, and the car was thrown into the path of a sixteen-wheeler. She was pronounced dead at the scene. She was only twenty-nine years old," he added flatly.

"That's terrible," Carrie said softly. "You must have been very young at the time."

"Five. Well, almost. My fifth birthday was three weeks after her funeral. I still remember blowing out the candles on my birthday cake while everyone told me to make a wish." He shrugged. "Helluva thing to say to a little kid whose mother just died. Of course, I wished that she would come back. And, of course, she didn't."

"Do you have any memories of her?"

"A few. They're mostly fleeting images rather than actual memories. I've looked at her pictures and tried to remember more." He looked at the triplets, then back at Carrie. "Maybe they're luckier not to have known their father at all. At least they didn't have to cope with losing him. Those were bad times for my brothers and me. Really bad times."

"It would be devastating for a child to lose his mother," Carrie said quietly. She thought of the mournful spiritual about the motherless child and the sense of abandonment and despair it evoked. And then she thought of five-year-old Tyler celebrating the first birthday of his life without his mother in it, of his innocent attempt to wish her back.

"Oh, Tyler, I'm so sorry." Impulsively, she put her arms around him and hugged him. It seemed the natural way to offer comfort to the lost, lonely child he had been.

Tyler hesitated for a moment, then wrapped his arms around her. "It's all right," he said quietly. "It happened a long, long time ago and there is no more grief. All I feel now is a vague sense of curiosity about what might have been had the accident not occurred."

"That's probably the way the triplets will feel about Ian," Carrie said sadly. "How could it be otherwise? Poor Ian. He deserved to be known and loved by his children."

"I'm sorry that they'll never know their father," murmured Tyler. His lips brushed the top of her silky blond hair. Once again, his senses began to spin.

Carrie closed her eyes and instinctively snuggled closer. Her motives had been to ease the pain of his inner child, but her body was responding to the man he had become. It felt so good to hold him and be held. Her hands smoothed over the broad bareness of his back, and she felt his arms tighten around her.

"Hi, Carrie! I thought I'd come over and—" Alexa gasped and stopped dead at the threshold of the kitchen.

Carrie and Tyler, who had been so absorbed in each other that they hadn't heard Alexa enter the house, self-consciously broke apart to face her. Alexa's blue eyes were round as saucers, her mouth comically agape as she stared at the pair.

Carrie blushed scarlet. She was suddenly aware of how skimpily she and Tyler were dressed—she in her swimsuit, he in his cutoff jeans. Through her sister's eyes, she saw the picture she and Tyler had presented, and she winced.

"We—I—didn't hear you come in, Lex," Carrie said weakly.

"Well, that's certainly obvious." Alexa sniffed.

"You didn't see what you thought you did," Tyler added quickly. "That is, what you saw isn't what you think."

He grimaced, feeling unjustly tried and accused. His embrace with Carrie had been perfectly innocent, two friends offering each other comfort and sympathy. But the way Alexa was staring at him made him feel as guilty as an adolescent caught necking in the park by a flashlight-toting cop. "Oh, hell," he muttered.

"Oh, hell!" Baby Dylan broke the silence, imitating Tyler perfectly, right down to the inflection.

"Don't react," Carrie cautioned quickly. "He'll forget it if he doesn't get a reaction. But if we laugh or make a big deal out of it—"

"—they'll all pick it up," Tyler concluded. "This trio loves an audience." He walked over to Dylan's high chair and swiped a grape from the tray. "Yikes, Dylan!" he said jovially.

"Yikes!" Dylan repeated, popping a grape into his own mouth. He grinned happily at Tyler.

Tyler grinned back. "Kids are so easy, once you get the knack," he said smugly. He saw Carrie and Alexa exchange glances. It was obvious that Alexa was dying to get her sister alone so she could grill her—probably lecture her, too—about what she'd seen when she'd barged in on them.

"Carrie, can I talk to you?" Alexa asked, confirming his supposition.

"I assume that's my cue to leave," Tyler said, deciding then and there that he was not going to be run off. Instead, he sat down at the table and resumed eating his sandwich.

"You missed your cue," Carrie pointed out dryly.

"Yeah, I guess I did." Tyler shrugged. "I don't take direction well. Good thing I'm not an actor."

Carrie and Alexa sat down, too. There seemed no point in hovering over the table while Tyler blithely consumed his lunch.

"I figured that you didn't get much sleep last night with that ungodly racket going on next door, Carrie," Alexa said as she fixed herself a sandwich. "I came over to watch the kids so you could lie down and get some rest this afternoon." She reached over and tousled Franklin's blond hair. "Besides, I miss the little devils. I'm used to spending almost every Sunday with them."

"Alexa watches the kids on the weekends I work and stays over during the day so I can sleep between shifts," Carrie explained to Tyler.

"Yeah, you told me that last night," he replied.

"Last night?" Alexa echoed suspiciously.

"I was over here last night, helping Carrie dispose of a body," Tyler whispered confidentially.

"Ignore him," Carrie advised the visibly flummoxed Alexa. "You can't take him seriously. He's a big teaser, even worse than Ben."

"Speaking of Ben..." Alexa lowered her voice and leaned forward in her chair. "I called him this morning to ask if he wanted to come over here with me, and he was not alone. It seems he met this woman named *Rhandee* at your neighbor's party last night." She shot Tyler a baleful look. "And the two of them ended up at his place."

"Ben hooked up with Rhandee? No kidding?" Tyler's curiosity was mildly piqued. Not his jealousy, though.

He frowned. Yesterday he had toyed with the idea of spending the night with Rhandee himself. Therefore, wasn't it reasonable to expect that he'd feel at least a twinge of jealousy at the thought of uninhibited, adventurous Rhandee with another man?

But he felt nothing. His eyes connected with Carrie's. Tyler stiffened. Merely gazing into those incomparable blue eyes of hers affected him more than any salacious fantasy of sexy, available Rhandee.

Unnerved, he had to struggle to play it cool. "So how did brother Ben survive his night with Rhandee? Or didn't he have enough energy left to talk about it?" He prided himself on hitting just the right glib note.

"Why don't you ask Ben yourself?" Carrie suggested sweetly. "I'll give you his number and you can call him and compare notes."

"And on that note of not-so-subtle censure, I think I'll take my leave." Tyler swallowed the last bite of his sandwich and rose to his feet. Oh, yes, it was definitely time to go.

He exited quickly through the back porch, amidst a wild chorus of "bye-bye" from the children. Carrie and Alexa looked at each other for a long moment.

"One question, Carrie. Do you know what you're doing?" Alexa frowned her concern. "What in the world is going on between you and Tyler Tremaine?"

"That's two questions," Carrie pointed out. "But I'll answer them both. I'm not doing anything, and there is nothing between Tyler and me. He was bored with his friends and his party, so he came over here. That's all."

"You were in his arms, Carrie," Alexa reminded her. "And he was in yours. What was that—an antidote to boredom?"

Carrie shrugged and studied the patterned weave of the place mat on the table. She found it difficult to meet her sister's probing blue eyes. "We'd been talking—" She paused and inhaled deeply, reluctant to share the confidences she and Tyler had exchanged. "We talked about losing people close to us and how the loss has affected us. He was only a child when his mother died. She was killed in a car accident in her twenties, just like Ian."

"Carrie, if you need to talk about losing Ian and how the loss is affecting your life, may I recommend that you do it at a meeting of Parents Without Partners or some other established support group? *Not* with a man like Tyler Tremaine!"

"He's actually a pretty nice guy when you get to know him, Alexa."

Alexa rolled her eyes. "Carrie, you don't know the man. You've seen the act he's decided to put on for you. His type won't let women close enough to know them, although they're quite willing to use portions of their history to their own advantage. I imagine he gets a lot of mileage out of his mother's tragic death. Everybody's heart bleeds for a poor little motherless child."

Carrie flushed, recalling her own heartfelt reaction to little Tyler's sad plight.

"Uh-huh. He got to you, didn't he?" Alexa nodded knowingly. "He probably has a script that he follows. I wonder what his next revelation will be. Maybe a heart-wrenching tale of a beloved little dog that ran away? Or worse, the beloved little dog is given away by unfeeling relatives—a coldhearted father, a wicked stepmother.''

"You're very cynical, Alexa." Carrie began scooping ice cream into three plastic bowls to serve to the children. "I seriously doubt that Tyler has some hidden agenda. Why would he bother? We're just friends."

"Friends, ha! Carrie, remember Ryan Cassidy?" Alexa demanded.

"Of course. He was a true rat, Alexa, but I think you've allowed the Ryan Cassidy experience to warp your judgment. Now you automatically assume *every* man is a slick, heartless, smooth operator just like him, and that's wrong, Alexa."

"Maybe. But you've had enough pain in your life, Carrie. I don't want you getting mixed up with a self-involved, manipulative snake who will break your heart."

As a certain self-involved, manipulative snake named Ryan Cassidy had broken Alexa's. Carrie gazed thoughtfully at her sister. There were all kinds of loss and all kinds of heartbreak. The kind that Alexa had experienced at the hands of Ryan Cassidy had changed her profoundly, darkening her outlook, robbing her of the ability to trust, leaving her bitter. Though losing Ian had been a terrible blow, it hadn't altered Carrie's view of the world and the people in it. She still believed in the power of love because she knew Ian had loved her and that he never would have voluntarily left her. It was a sustaining comfort, one denied to Alexa.

"Don't worry about me, Alexa. I'm not going to get involved with anybody," Carrie assured her sister. "Now, while we're waiting for the kids to finish their ice cream, tell me all about Ben and his latest flame."

"I'm furious with Ben for behaving like a predatory sleaze and I told him so," Alexa said, dipping her spoon into the ice-cream container. "We can't let our own brother turn into a calculating, coldhearted user like—like Ryan Cassidy, Carrie." She met her sister's eyes and held them. "Or Tyler Tremaine."

Carrie thought of those two burning kisses she and Tyler had shared, and went hot all over. She might not be well-versed in the ways of rakish cads, but she did know one thing: she hadn't been Tyler's innocent victim either time. She'd been a full and voluntary participant. If he was using her, then she had been using him, too.

Emily threw her empty bowl to the floor, announcing that the ice cream was "All gone!" An admiring Franklin followed Emily's lead, and Dylan was quick to imitate him. Carrie welcomed the diversion. She didn't care for the direction her thoughts had taken. It was a relief to redirect them.

The two sisters turned their attention to the babies and the task of getting them cleaned up and out of the high chairs and into their cribs for their afternoon naps. The name of Tyler Tremaine was not mentioned again for the rest of the day.

The temperature climbed into the mid-nineties, unseasonably hot for Washington. Even though he'd spent most of the day in air-conditioned buildings, driving to and from in his air-conditioned car, the first thing Tyler did upon arriving home was to strip, shower and change into a loose, comfortable old pair of khaki shorts and an equally old striped cotton shirt.

He glanced at his watch; it read 7:42. His dinner meeting had ended far earlier than he had planned. The client had a family he was eager to get home to and passed on Tyler's invitation to extend the evening with drinks or a festive round of the area clubs. The Tremaines were known for their flair and largess when it came to wooing prospective clients or keeping current ones happy.

But here he was, home unexpectedly early on Monday evening, hours of free time stretching before him. There were any number of people, both male and female, he could call who would be glad to see him, who would drop whatever they were doing to do whatever he proposed doing. And there were any number of things he could propose to do.

But not a single one of the myriad of activities or pastimes that came to mind held any interest or appeal for him tonight. He leafed through his Rolodex file—he kept one at home and one in the office so he would never be caught without his contacts—and methodically rejected every single name he read.

Clutching a paper bag imprinted with the Tremaine Drugs logo, he slipped quietly out the back door, heading for the gap in the hedge separating the lush greenery of his property from Carrie Wilcox's unimpressive backyard.

He didn't bother to ask himself what he was doing or why. When there were no answers, it was best to sidestep the questions.

Carrie was in the kitchen, pouring herself a tall glass of iced tea, when Tyler appeared at the door. A blast of warm air from the oscillating fan on the counter ruffled her hair as she opened the door to him.

"Hi." Her smile was incandescent, lighting her whole face; her blue eyes glowed with warmth. Tyler stared at her, momentarily mesmerized. Her hair was pulled off her neck into a short, high ponytail, and she was wearing a turquoise cotton shift, loose and short and sleeveless.

He felt curiously light-headed and it was suddenly difficult to speak. "I, uh—Look what I found in one of our stores today." He pulled a rubber duck out of the paper bag. It was identical to the duck that had sparked Dylan and Franklin's scuffle in the pool yesterday.

"I was visting the Wheaton store—I make rounds of all the area stores every few months—and I spied this duck in the toy aisle." Tyler reached into the bag and pulled out a second identical duck. "So I bought two of them. Now each of the kids has a duck. Three kids, three ducks."

Now that he'd begun talking, he couldn't seem to stop. "I thought about what you'd said, about wanting the kids to be friends, not rivals. It makes sense. I mean, it's certainly happier for all concerned if brothers are pals instead of beating the hell out of each other, right?"

"Right." Carrie smiled. "And thank you for the ducks, the kids will love them. It was very thoughtful of you, Tyler."

He handed her the bag. "Where are the tiny terrors, anyway? It's awfully quiet around here."

"They're in bed."

He glanced at his watch. "So early? It's not even eight o'clock."

"Their bedtime is seven-thirty. They talk and play in their cribs for a little while before they finally settle down, so maybe they're still awake. Do you want to go upstairs and see?"

"No, that's not necessary." He leaned against the doorjamb. "So you have some free time without the munchkins underfoot? What are you planning to do?"

Carrie shrugged. "There's a lineup of shows I usually watch on TV tonight." She named them.

Tyler drew a blank. "I seldom watch television," he confessed. "And when I do, it's to watch the commercials for programs that Tremaine Incorporated is sponsoring or to keep up my end of the conversation with clients who advertise on certain shows and want to talk about them."

"So for you, watching TV is work, not relaxation. For me, it's a chance to sit down and unwind. I enjoy it." Carrie glanced at the kitchen clock. "I'm going to make some popcorn before the shows start."

They never actually discussed his joining her to watch television. But when she carried the bowl of popcorn into the living room and switched on the TV set, he was right behind her. They sat down together, side by side, on the sofa.

The room was dark and stuffy. Tyler leaned back against the cushions. "I thought old Mr. Wilcox had central air-conditioning in this place."

"No. There's a window air-conditioning unit in the kids' room, but that's the only one in the house. Ben says he has a lead on a secondhand one for my bedroom, but until I buy it, I make do with fans."

"Well, the fan in this room isn't doing any good. You have to sit here and wait while it oscillates, then lean forward to catch the breeze for a second or two when it finally comes your way." Tyler felt hot, sticky and irritable. Oppressive heat always affected him this way.

Carrie tucked her feet under her and watched the TV screen, occasionally reaching into the bowl for a handful of popcorn. Tyler shifted restlessly. It was ridiculous for him to be here, sweating and bored by an inane sitcom, when he had a state-of-the-art entertainment center in his house. His cool, comfortable, air-conditioned house.

He made a few derogatory comments about the heat, then a few more about the program on television, becoming particularly offended when a rival drugstore chain aired a schmaltzy commercial, complete with sentimental music, dogs, children and senior citizens.

"That's an example of a shamelessly manipulative advertising ploy that has absolutely nothing to do with selling anything in a drugstore!" he railed at the set.

"But it does grab your interest," Carrie remarked. "And I thought it was sweet when the grandma bought ice-cream cones for the little boy and the baby and the dog."

"That drugstore chain doesn't even sell ice cream!" snapped Tyler. "Tremaine Drugs has lower prices, more efficient service—"

"And really boring commercials," Carrie inserted playfully.

"Boring? *Boring!* Our commercials are first rate—informative, unpretentious, aimed at the consumer's brain and his pocketbook, not his heartstrings. Lord knows we spend enough on advertising to—"

"I was only kidding," Carrie cut in. "I'm sure your commercials are everything you said they are."

That was not the response the company's executive vice-president and head of marketing wanted to hear. "My opinion of our commercials is of no consequence. It's the consumers—TV viewers like yourself—whom we're trying to reach, and I *thought* our ads were effective. We've done marketing surveys that show—"

"Shh. The program's back on." Carrie turned her attention back to the screen, clearly uninterested in Tremaine Incorporated's marketing surveys.

Tyler was insulted. The last time he'd been shushed had been . . . Why, he couldn't remember the last time. Maybe it had never happened before. People tended to hang on his every word; his views and opinions were sought and admired and even *quoted!* Furthermore, he'd never spent a whole evening sitting in front of the tube watching network television in his life! And to have to endure it in a room so hot it seemed to prove the greenhouse effect was simply intolerable.

He stood up. "I'm leaving."

Carrie's eyes never left the screen. "'Bye, Tyler. Thanks again for the ducks."

"You don't care if I leave or not," Tyler accused.

At last she looked away from the television and stared up at him with her big blue eyes. "You're welcome to stay but since you're miserable here, it's better that you go."

"Do you want me to stay or not?" he snapped.

"Well, yes, I would like you to stay, but only if you want to," she said slowly, choosing her words very carefully, as if dealing with an unpredictable, explosive psychotic.

Tyler was incensed. "Stop patronizing me!"

"I wasn't. I said I'd like you to stay."

"Then say it like you mean it. Make me want to stay!"

Carrie's eyes widened. Make him want to stay. She reached for the bowl of popcorn and held it up to him. "Um, have some," she offered.

Tyler's sense of humor got the better of him. "How can I resist an offer like that?" He laughed, though he was aware that his predicament was certainly no laughing matter. *He was about to choose to remain here in this inferno, watching her watch TV!*

He sank back down on the sofa, heaving a sigh of self-exasperation.

"Tyler, may I ask you something?" Carrie said tentatively.

"Sure."

She frowned uneasily. "Did you ever have a dog when you were a boy?"

"No, and I never wanted one, either. The closest I ever came to having a pet was leaving food outside for that maniacal Psycho-Kitty, and that's as close as I ever plan to get."

"Sleuth is upstairs sleeping on my bed right now," Carrie said, using the name she had given her adopted cat. She was inordinately relieved that Alexa was wrong and there would be no calculated sob story about a beloved little dog. "That cat loves the heat. It can never get too hot for him," she added cheerfully.

"Yeah, well, I told you he was crazy. But probably no crazier than I am at this point." And with that, Tyler reached for her with both hands and yanked her onto his lap.

Six

He'd scooped her up as easily as he lifted little Emily, simply plucking her from one spot and placing her in another, proving his greater strength and physical power over her. Common sense told Carrie that she had cause to be concerned. She was a woman alone with a much bigger, much stronger man whom she really didn't know all that well.

But she felt no fear, not even a twinge of anxiety. Some intuitive insight assured her that she was not at risk, that she was safe with Tyler. As safe as she wanted to be. That renegade thought streaked through her head, startling her as much as her unexpected seat on Tyler's lap.

She turned her head to look at him, and their gazes locked.

Tyler stared into the blue depths of her eyes. His bad mood had completely evaporated. Suddenly the heat wasn't so unbearable anymore and the sound of the TV laugh track no longer made him want to commit mayhem. With his one hand resting on the curve of her hip and the other on her thigh, he could feel the warmth of her skin through the soft turquoise cotton of her dress. He felt his body tighten and begin to throb with pure sensual pleasure. He'd wanted this....

The sexual tension radiated between them. Carrie felt the need to break the charged silence. "Do you do this often?" she murmured.

Tyler kept his arms around her, pleased that she had made no attempt to get up, because he doubted that he would've let her. It was something of a revelation to discover that he harbored such Neanderthal instincts. They'd certainly never surfaced before.

"Do I do what often?" He feigned ignorance, stalling for time.

"That particular move of yours which landed me here on your lap," she said bluntly.

Tyler winced. He was all out of time. "It wasn't a move, it was more like a lunge," he admitted grudgingly. "And quite unlike me. Normally, I'm smooth and sophisticated. Subtle. I've been complimented often on my superb technique. Not this time, though." He grimaced wryly. "There wasn't a hint of subtlety displayed here. I pounced on you the way Psycho-Kitty pounces on small prey."

"Sleuth doesn't hunt anymore," Carrie assured him. "He has a home and a family now and he no longer roams. His hunting days are over."

"Hmm, I doubt it. I think he's only experimenting with domesticity and will revert to his wild ways when he grows bored."

Carrie shook her head. "His transformation is complete. Time will prove me right, you'll see."

Tyler sighed impatiently. "Are we going to talk about that stupid cat all night?"

"What would you rather talk about? Tremaine's marketing surveys?" Carrie teased, her blue eyes sparkling. "Now there's an infinitely fascinating subject." Without pausing to think about it, she slipped her arms around Tyler's neck, holding him as loosely and casually as he was holding her. She felt relaxed with him, yet at the same time excitement was churning through her.

"I think I'd rather not talk at all," Tyler said tautly. He shifted his legs, causing her to sink back against him, more deeply in his embrace.

Once more, her eyes met his. Carrie felt lost in his deep green gaze. Her head began to spin. He had such beautiful eyes, she thought dizzily. Such a sexy, irresistible mouth. Her hand crept up to trace the outline of his lips with her fingertips. She forgot to invoke her memories of Ian; she forgot everything except the feverish rush of need coursing through her.

Tyler gently kneaded the curve of thigh and the soft swell of her belly through the soft cotton. He nuzzled her neck, kissing, nibbling, tasting her skin, his fingers caressing, his hands growing more possessive.

A flood of sensual heat suffused her. Carrie was a little worried by the unexpected intensity of the pleasure rippling through her. But she liked what he was doing so much that she wanted it to go on and on. Her eyelids drifted shut as she tilted her head back to give him greater access to the slender curve of her throat. She was achingly aware of his big hand inching up toward her breast.

Tyler's mouth closed over hers, hot and hard and hungry, and Carrie shivered as an electrifying jolt of desire flashed through her. Her lips parted on a soft moan and she arched against him, her fingers threading in the dark thickness of his hair. His tongue plunged deeply into her mouth, filling her with one hot thrust, then probed and claimed the soft moist warmth within.

Carrie's heart slammed against her ribcage in double time and she whimpered against his boldly ardent mouth. Her thoughts were splintering. She knew they shouldn't be doing this, but she couldn't bear to end it.

"You're holding back," Tyler said raspily. "Kiss me the way you did before." The memory of those soul-shattering kisses added fuel to the hot flames burning inside him. Like an addict, he craved more. "Put your tongue in my mouth," he demanded. Having experienced the full range of her passionate response, he couldn't settle for anything less.

His explicit sensual directions excited her. She felt a wholly feminine, voluptuous need to give to him—and an equally strong desire to take the passion that he offered.

She leaned into him, and when his mouth closed protectively over hers again, Carrie gave in to his sensuous command. She claimed his mouth with her lips and her tongue, kissing him hotly, deeply, as she clung to him. Desire sliced through her, sharp and swift and shockingly pleasurable.

His hand cupped the soft fullness of her breast through the turquoise cotton, caressing the lush roundness, then gliding his thumb over the taut peak of her nipple. It strained against the material, visibly outlined through the cloth. Carrie's reaction was electrical. She jerked spasmodically, and a gasp escaped from her throat.

"You're very sensitive." Tyler's voice was a low, sexy growl that incited her further. "I knew you would be. Anyone as passionate and responsive as you would *have* to be... And the way you kiss...damn, you can kiss...." His voice trailed off. He was barely capable of uttering the free associations drifting through his passion-dazed mind.

His thumb carefully circled her nipple, making it throb with an ache she felt deep, deep inside her. His mouth played softly with hers, their breath mingling.

Carrie felt control slipping away, but she couldn't seem to summon the will to regain it. She didn't want to. Her hands slid over his shoulders, savoring the strong muscular feel of him. She wriggled sensuously on his lap and thrilled to the unbridled strength of his male arousal.

Tyler was staggered by the intensity of his feelings, by the force of his own need. He knew he could satisfy a woman and take his own pleasure—there were all those testimonials to his technique—but never had his blood drummed with this primitive urgency.

Breathing heavily, he bunched the material of her dress in his hand and shoved it up, sliding his fingers under it, along the silky soft skin of her thigh. His hand moved higher to the enticing curve of her buttocks, then lightly skimmed over her belly to the crevice between her legs. He felt the hot, damp silk, indisputable evidence that she wanted him, and caressed her through it. Her breath caught in a moan and she parted her legs, giving him freer access in an unspoken but unmistakable invitation.

Another wild surge of desire exploded through him. But he was allowed to linger in those thrilling heights for only a few moments.

"Tyler, no." Carrie pushed his hand away. She could still feel the imprint of his fingers, as if they'd been scorched on her skin. Between her thighs she was achy and swollen and acutely sensitive. But she forced herself to stand. "We have to stop this," she said breathlessly, quickly crossing the room.

"We don't have to stop," Tyler argued. Blood was roaring in his ears, and his body throbbed with raw need. "You don't want to stop and neither do I, Carrie. We're both—"

"You must think I—that I'm something of a slut," Carrie lamented, pacing back and forth in front of the fan. She needed to cool off, in more ways than one. Her body felt wired with a tense nervous energy, geared for a sexual release that would not be forthcoming. "I mean, how could you not? Considering my behavior, even *I* think I'm a slut."

Tyler sighed heavily. This was not a conversation he wanted to have. His body ached from a churning sexual frustration. He flexed his fingers, remembering her softness, wanting to feel it again. He nearly groaned aloud at the potent, tactile memory. But first things first. "You're not a slut, Carrie."

His words gave her no solace. "You would say that, of course. What else could you say?" The speed of her pacing picked up. "You're too smooth and sophisticated—too subtle—to tell the truth."

Tyler closed his eyes. "Obviously, I'm not as smooth or sophisticated or subtle as I thought or my own words wouldn't be coming back to haunt me."

"To have this happen, after all the things we said yesterday—" Carrie broke off, distraught. Her own body had turned traitor, overriding all her fine sentiments and noble aspirations to pursue a purely physical agenda, featuring sex as the headliner.

Tyler tried to remember what they'd said yesterday. His mind was clouded with unsatisfied passion, his powers of recollection severely limited. "Will you please sit down," he said, groaning. "You're moving in warp speed and it's giving me a headache."

"I betrayed Ian." Carrie paused only for a moment before resuming her pacing at double warp speed. Tonight's little episode on the couch had not been fueled by curiosity or compassion; she couldn't pretend otherwise. She'd wanted Tyler badly.

Worse, when she tried to recall if she'd ever felt such an overpowering, aching desire for Ian, she couldn't. More and more, Ian had become an ethereal image in her mind, saintlike and pure, far removed from anything as earthy and real as sexual thoughts and needs. Shame washed over her. "I betrayed Ian and I used you to do it. I'm sorry, Tyler. It was terrible of me."

Tyler stared at her. This was a first. "You're apologizing for using me?" he repeated carefully.

Carrie nodded, clearly distressed. She'd told him that she had neither the time nor interest nor energy to become sexually involved with anyone and she had believed it when she'd said it. But her own actions belied her words. She was certainly acting as if she was ready, willing and able to become involved with him!

Never had her mind and her body been so far apart, her values and her needs clashing in a no-win struggle. "I love Ian, yet I—"

"Carrie, a few kisses and some very light petting does not, in my mind, constitute betrayal."

Her cheeks flamed. He had already categorized and dismissed as trivial the explosive passion that had rocked her quiet little world. She felt embarrassed, hurt and resentful, and searched her mind for just the right words to make him feel the same.

Tyler mistook her silence for doubt. "Carrie, Ian is dead!" He tried to mask the exasperation and frustration coursing through him, but wasn't sure how well he succeeded. "You loved the man but he's not around anymore for you to betray. The marriage vows say 'till death do you part,' right? Well, death parted you. Your vow is now null and void."

Carrie seemed to freeze in place. Tyler watched the color drain from her face, saw her blue eyes fill with tears. He scowled darkly. Now he'd done it! He felt like a heartless bully, much the same way he'd felt when he had snatched the toy duck from Dylan and Franklin and watched their small faces crumple into tears.

But what he'd said was true, Tyler assured himself, and Carrie needed to hear it. However painful, she had to face the fact that her needs and feelings had not died with her husband. He rose to his feet and came to stand beside her. A gust of wind from the fan blew in his face.

"Carrie, don't cry." It was a plea and an order combined.

"I'm not going to." Carrie blinked her tears back, determined that they wouldn't fall. "I hate crying," she said fiercely. "I take pride in the fact that I haven't cried since the

Here are your BIG WIN Game Tickets potentially worth from $100.00 to $1,000,000.00 each. Scratch off the PINK METALLIC STRIP on each of your Sweepstakes tickets to see what you could win and mail your entry right away. (SEE OFFICIAL RULES IN BACK OF BOOK FOR DETAILS!)

This could be your lucky day - GOOD LUCK!

FOLD AND DETACH ALONG THIS DOTTED LINE—RETURN ALL GAME TICKETS INTACT.

TICKET 1
THE BIG WIN
Scratch PINK METALLIC STRIP to reveal potential value of this ticket if it is a winning ticket. Return all game tickets intact.

LUCKY NUMBER

1P 820215

TICKET 2
THE BIG WIN
Scratch PINK METALLIC STRIP to reveal potential value of this ticket if it is a winning ticket. Return all game tickets intact.

LUCKY NUMBER

4Y 820215

TICKET 3
THE BIG WIN
Scratch PINK METALLIC STRIP to reveal potential value of this ticket if it is a winning ticket. Return all game tickets intact.

LUCKY NUMBER

3Q 820215

TICKET 4
THE BIG WIN
Scratch PINK METALLIC STRIP to reveal potential value of this ticket if it is a winning ticket. Return all game tickets intact.

LUCKY NUMBER

9T 820215

TICKET 5
FREE BOOKS
We're giving away brand new books to selected individuals. Scratch PINK METALLIC STRIP for number of free books you will receive.

AUTHORIZATION CODE

130107-742

TICKET 6
FREE GIFT
We have an outstanding added gift for you if you are accepting our free books. Scratch PINK METALLIC STRIP to reveal gift.

AUTHORIZATION CODE

130107-742

YES! Enter my Lucky Numbers in THE BIG WIN Sweepstakes and when winners are selected, tell me if I've won any prize. If the PINK METALLIC STRIP is scratched off on ticket #5, I will also receive one or more FREE Silhouette Desire® novels along with the FREE GIFT on ticket #6, as explained on the back and on the opposite page.

225 CIS AH76 (U-SIL-D-06/93)

NAME _____

ADDRESS _____ APT. _____

CITY _____ STATE _____ ZIP CODE _____

Book offer limited to one per household and not valid to current Silhouette Desire subscribers. All orders subject to approval.

BUSINESS REPLY MAIL
FIRST CLASS MAIL   PERMIT NO. 717   BUFFALO, NY

POSTAGE WILL BE PAID BY ADDRESSEE

SILHOUETTE READER SERVICE
3010 WALDEN AVE
PO BOX 1867
BUFFALO NY 14240-9952

NO POSTAGE
NECESSARY
IF MAILED
IN THE
UNITED STATES

triplets were born. Oh, my eyes may fill up, I might feel like crying, but I force myself not to."

Her firm little declaration affected Tyler more than if she'd burst into tears. "Maybe it would be easier on you if you let yourself cry once in awhile," he said quietly, astonished by what he was advocating. Women's tears made him uncomfortable; at the first sign of a sob or a sniffle, he fled the scene.

Carrie shook his head. "No, crying doesn't solve anything." She smiled a little, more confident and in control once again. "Your eyes get red and puffy, your nose runs, and you look ugly. No, thanks, I'll pass on crying."

Tyler studied her averted profile—the sweep of her long dark lashes, her soft lips and firm little chin—and a peculiar feeling, one that he was quite unfamiliar with, swept through him. "Carrie, you couldn't look ugly if you tried," he said huskily.

Impulsively, compulsively, he reached out to cup her cheek with his hand.

"Thanks, but I know otherwise." Carrie quickly stepped away, out of touching distance. She felt awkward and exhausted, out of her depth. She wanted him to go. "It's getting late," she said, glancing pointedly at her wristwatch.

"Yeah, real late. Nine o'clock," Tyler reported sardonically. "It always seems to come down to this, doesn't it? You kicking me out."

"There's no reason for you to stay."

Her rejection stung, far more than it should have. "You're right. There is absolutely no reason for me to hang around here." He headed to the front door, Carrie a few feet behind him, presumably to make sure that he left.

The door opened as he stepped into the small, dark vestibule. Tyler found himself face-to-face with Ben Shaw, who looked astonished to see him there.

"What's wrong?" Ben demanded, looking from Tyler to Carrie. "Are the kids okay? Are you okay, Carrie?"

"Everything's fine, Ben," Carrie assured him. "Tyler dropped by with some things from the drugstore. He was just leaving," she added in a not-so-subtle hint for him to do just that.

"Hey, no need to rush off!" Ben exclaimed. "Carrie, why don't you get us something cold to drink and we'll all—"

"I already gave him a glass of iced tea," Carrie said flatly. "He drank it and now he wants to go. It's too hot for him here. He's used to air-conditioning and he breaks out in a heat rash without it."

"Heat rash?" Tyler echoed indignantly. She'd made him sound like some kind of wimp!

"It's nothing to be ashamed of, man," consoled Ben. "Could happen to anybody."

"Well, it's never happened to me!" Tyler started toward the door. But he paused on the threshold, turning to Ben. "I understand you spent the rest of the weekend with Rhandee. How'd it go?"

He watched Carrie's face flush with anger, saw the blue fire in her eyes and smiled in satisfaction. He had known she wouldn't like his interest in Rhandee's adventure with Ben, and though he was committed to leaving as quickly as possible, he hadn't been able to pass up that one sure shot at needling her.

"Rhandee." Ben fairly sighed the name. "Oh, God, it was great. She was great." Then his blissful smile turned into a scowl and he looked purposefully at Carrie. "Which brings me to the reason why I'm here, Carrie. Will you please tell your sister that I'm old enough to run my own life and that I don't appreciate her interference or her lectures? Tell her to give me a break and keep her nose out of my business!"

"*My* sister?" Carrie couldn't suppress a smile. "It's that bad, huh?"

"It's worse." Ben groaned. "Alexa went ballistic when she found out I went to bed with Rhandee the same night I met her. She—"

"Just for the record, how many hours did you two know each other before you hit the sack?" Tyler asked.

Carrie shot him a dark look. Ben sighed deeply. "I know you're only kidding, Tyler, but Alexa asked me the same question, and she wasn't! Since then she's been lecturing me about the hazards of sex and accusing me of acting like a no-class womanizing user like Ryan Cassidy—*Ryan Cassidy!*—when she knows how much I hate the guy and—"

"You're not like Ryan Cassidy, Ben," Carrie said soothingly.

"Do you mean Ryan Cassidy, the cartoonist?" Tyler asked at the same time.

Carrie and Ben exchanged glances, and Tyler was startled by the blatant hostility in both pairs of blue eyes.

"Cartoonist, ha!" Ben sneered. "His stories are witless. Why, he can't even draw! Some cartoonist!"

"His comic strip is very popular," Tyler pointed out. "He's been extremely successful with it. The annual collections of his daily strips are Tremaine Books' top sellers year after year."

"We don't buy them," Carrie said succinctly.

"I know his comic strips are controversial, but it sounds more like you two have a personal grudge against Cassidy," Tyler said, his curiosity roused.

"There's bad blood between us," Ben admitted. "Not to mention a whole lot of sugar, huh, Carrie?" He winked at Carrie. She gave her head a warning shake.

Ben obviously thought he was being cunningly oblique, but Tyler's eyes widened in instant comprehension. "Someone poured a pound of sugar into the gas tank of Cassidy's red 1964 Ford Thunderbird convertible a couple years ago. I'd been trying to talk him into selling me that beauty for ages, but he never would. The sugar totally destroyed the engine, the car was devalued and—''

"It wasn't devalued, it was ruined," Ben corrected.

"And you did it, didn't you?" Tyler stared at him, shocked. "You were responsible for deliberately ruining that beautiful, classic car! But why?"

"Ben, don't say anything more," Carrie warned.

Ben ignored her. "Cassidy is a cold-blooded creep who deliberately broke Alexa's heart," he blurted out. "It's only fair that he should suffer the same kind of pain he caused her, but since he has no heart, we had to settle for—"

"Destroying his car," Tyler concluded. He looked hard at Carrie. "Were you in on it, too?"

Ben shook his head, answering for her. "Carrie and Alexa didn't know anything until afterwards, when I told them. I acted on my own," he added rather proudly.

Carrie read the disapproval and disgust in Tyler's eyes as he stared at Ben. The full force of her sisterly loyalty rose to the fore. How dare Tyler Tremaine judge Ben when he didn't know how much Ben cared nor how terribly Alexa had suffered!

"Ryan Cassidy is a cold, arrogant weasel who deserved much worse for the way he treated Alexa," she said, coming to Ben's defense.

"Ah, but why stop at wrecking the guy's prize car?" Tyler countered sarcastically. He'd been irate when he had heard of the car's destruction; he felt the same way now. A masterpiece had been destroyed! "Why didn't you chop off his hands? A definite setback for a cartoonist but a fitting revenge for the unspeakable crime of dumping your sister."

"We don't expect you to understand," Carrie murmured tightly.

"I understand that if sugar ever turns up in the gas tanks of any of my cars, I'll know who to file charges against," Tyler called over his shoulder as he strode swiftly from the house. He couldn't get away fast enough! He promised himself that he would *not* be back.

"Now he thinks we're demented," Ben said plaintively.

Carrie refused to acknowledge the niggling pain inside her. "It doesn't matter what he thinks, Ben."

"It does matter, Carrie. He's a *Tremaine!* Think of the advantages if he were to take a liking to us, if he respected us! I have this terrific idea for a whole new ad campaign for Tremaine Drugs, including a can't-miss TV commercial. I started working on it the day I met Tyler, right here in your house. If I can sell it to Tremaine Incorporated, it's my ticket out of that dead-end broom closet I'm stuck in, Carrie."

"I don't think Tyler's going to be too eager to listen, Ben," Carrie warned. "Particularly not now."

"I guess it was a mistake to confess to sugaring Ryan Cassidy's red T-bird convertible to a classic-car nut," Ben concluded regretfully. "Good thing he doesn't know about the rest of the revenge. Carrie, will you do me a favor? If for any reason, Tremaine happens to drop by again, will you try to—"

"Use my considerable influence with him to get you an appointment to present your advertising ideas?" Carrie grimaced sardonically. "Ben, you'd have better luck trying to get to him through your mutual friend Rhandee."

"He did seem interested in her, didn't he?" Ben said thoughtfully. "I think he really wanted to talk about her. Damn, it's too bad we got off on that Ryan Cassidy tangent. Hey, where are you going, Carrie?"

"Upstairs to take a shower," she replied. Where she could avoid discussing Tyler Tremaine's interest in the legendary Rhandee. "You're welcome to stick around and watch TV, Ben."

"Okay. I think I'll make a phone call first, though."

"To Alexa?" Carrie suggested.

"Heck, no!" Ben grinned. "To Rhandee."

For the next three days, whenever he had a spare moment, Tyler reminded himself of the fate which awaited the defenseless cars of those who happened to rile one of the vengeful Shaw triplets. He pictured himself turning the ignition key in one of the classic cars in his prized collection and sending a fatal spurt of sugar into the engine. It was a dreadful specter. He congratulated himself on escaping the triplets' acquaintanceship with his property, person and possessions intact.

His hours at the office were, as always, an endless continuum of meetings, phone calls, paperwork. He might be a Tremaine heir, but he was also the aspiring president of the company, dedicated to the progress and profit of Tremaine Incorporated. According to the unspoken yet consensual family plan, when their father retired, Cole would take over as chairman and Tyler would advance to the presidency. He intended his eventual promotion to be earned and inevitable, through his hard work, not his bloodlines.

Out of the office, he wined and dined clients one night and the next evening attended a trade association's cocktail-and-dinner party where he effectively represented Tremaine Incorporated with all his well-practiced charm.

Upon returning home late both nights, he paused in his driveway and stared at the corner house next door. It was completely dark inside. The only illumination came from the low-wattage porch light. Obviously, Carrie and her toddler triplets were sleeping.

And as he sat in his car, staring down into the darkness, an image of Carrie smiling up at him, her wide blue eyes shining with warmth, flashed before his mind's eye. It was an incredible three-dimensional, sensory image because he could hear her laugh, feel the softness of her skin beneath his hands, smell the clean, fresh scent of her soft, pale hair.

The ability to conjure her up so vividly was not limited to his waking hours. It extended into his dreams. . . .

They were lying together, kissing, and her small, delicate hands were caressing him, innocently at first, then delving lower in increasingly bold strokes. He groaned with pleasure, then returned the favor, smoothing his palms over her rounded breasts that felt so soft and full in his hands. He kissed the tight pink tips until she moaned her arousal, then pulled her down for another slow, deep kiss that seemed to go on forever. His fingertips skimmed the soft nest between her thighs, then probed deeper into her feminine heat, feeling her wetness, knowing it was all for him. She murmured something sexy and intimate in his ear, words that inflamed him even further. His heart was pounding, his blood flowing thickly, and when her fingers closed around the pulsing, throbbing heat of him, he called her name.

"Carrie!" He spoke it aloud, awakening himself.

Tyler sat up in bed, perspiring despite the cool thermostat setting, his pulses still pounding, his erection hard as stone. He'd been dreaming, the kind of sex dream he hadn't had for years. He'd had no need of nighttime fantasy when his real life provided him with the satisfaction and release his body craved. At least, it had until now. Now, he was suffering from sexual frustration and deprivation, paying the price for those all-too-brief, passionate interludes that Carrie had halted with rather insulting ease.

It was definitely time to remedy the situation. He couldn't handle hot dreams and cold showers in the middle of the night. He didn't have to, not Tyler Tremaine! He decided to act on the message his body was sending him and direct his attention to his sex life, which certainly had been lacking lately. Actually, it had been nonexistent. But that unfortunate situation was about to end.

It was drinks, a show, dinner and a nightcap at a trendy, smoky little jazz club, with an attractive young woman named Gwenda who listened raptly as he talked about himself, giggling delightedly at all his jokes. She even giggled when he wasn't joking, but Tyler didn't mind. At least she didn't scold him or tell him to get lost like certain other women he could name. Like one certain woman whose name and face kept springing to mind despite his best efforts to banish her from his thoughts.

He was pleased when Gwenda offered to extend the evening with an invitation to her apartment. There was soft music, soft lights and an air conditioner humming away the heat and humidity. She poured him a glass of wine and sat close beside him on the black leather couch.

The signals were unmistakable. It was an all-systems-go clearance, and time for him to make a move. When he hesitated, she made the move. And that's when he knew for certain that it just wasn't going to work.

Tyler was thoroughly disconcerted. It had seemed so simple. He would assuage his body's raging desire with the sexual release it craved. After all, sex was a drive, a basic instinct. If he were starving, he would gladly eat whatever was offered, be it gourmet fare or—a marshmallow pudding confection. So why was his body sabotaging his attempt to end the sexual famine plaguing him? What had happened to his rampant arousal?

When Gwenda offered him sympathy and expressed understanding for his "problem," his humiliation was complete. He left immediately, arriving home to see every light in Carrie's house blazing, a striking contrast from past nights, when the place was dark as a tomb at this hour.

He was not an alarmist, Tyler assured himself, deciding at the same time that something was definitely not right next door. He left his car in his driveway and strode to Carrie's front door, rapping the old brass knocker sharply.

"Who's there?" Carrie's anxious voice quavered from the other side.

"It's Tyler. Open the door, Carrie."

She recognized his voice and opened the door at once. Tyler stood before her, obviously dressed for a night on the town. His attire left no doubt of that. She stared at him, her blue eyes both admiring and puzzled. Whether in cutoff jeans or full date regalia, he was an indisputably marvelous-looking man. But what on earth was he doing on her doorstep at three o'clock in the morning?

"Is—is there something wrong?" she asked tentatively.

"I came over here to ask *you* that question." Tyler couldn't take his eyes from her.

She was wearing a short little robe of blue silky material that matched and enhanced her already-too-entrancing blue eyes. The robe was belted with a thin blue sash whose knot did not look all that sturdy. One swift pull and the knot would be history; the robe would fall open, exposing her to him. Tyler wondered what she was wearing under it. He wondered why and how he managed to keep catching her in nightclothes. Nightclothes that were invariably modest and unrevealing yet stimulated his imagination and his hormones to raging levels. It was an additional torment—just what he didn't need!—in this ongoing look-and-don't-touch game of theirs.

"This place is lit up like a Christmas tree," he said thickly. "You have every light in the place on."

"Not every light," Carrie countered. "The babies' room is dark. They're sleeping."

She fiddled with the sash of her robe while Tyler watched closely. Was the knot loosening? He peered hopefully.

Carrie felt the knot of her tie belt coming undone and quickly tightened it. Tyler was staring at her with those enigmatic green eyes of his. She had to remind herself to exhale.

"Do you want to come in?" she asked at last, her voice soft and a little uncertain.

Seven

Tyler did not want to come inside. Clearly, nothing was wrong here. He should go home and get some sleep and let Carrie get on with whatever it was she was doing at this hour. She certainly had enough light to do it by.

Instead he stepped inside, gripped by an ironic sense of the inevitable. It was as if he were a metal filing and she were a magnet. He was drawn to her, so attracted that he couldn't pull away. A humbling admission, particularly after tonight's fiasco with Gwenda. Worse, his traitorous body was tightening with unmistakable anticipation. The virile response which had defied Gwenda's amorous advances had been achieved effortlessly by merely looking at Carrie. Tyler broke into a sweat, and it wasn't due entirely to the lack of air-conditioning.

"What's going on, Carrie?" he asked roughly. "Why are you still up? It's three—"

"I know what time it is," Carrie interrupted. "I couldn't sleep, so I—"

"Put on every light, except in the children's room?" His voice deepened. "What's the matter, Carrie?"

"I have a bad, bad case of the creeps," Carrie said. She headed toward the kitchen and Tyler followed her, watching her open the old-fashioned wooden bread box that sat on the counter.

She took out a book. "I put this in here because even the sight of it bothers me," she confessed sheepishly. "Ben said it was a thriller. A real page-turner, he called it. I started to read it after I put the kids to bed and it scared me so much I couldn't sleep. I couldn't even turn off the lights."

Carrie looked at the cover and shuddered. "I'm not usually the nervous type, but this—" She gazed up at Tyler, her blue eyes wide. "It's about a brilliant, sadistic serial killer who breaks into houses at night and—"

"Just the sort of thing a young single mother who lives alone ought to read at bedtime," Tyler cut in caustically, frowning his disapproval. "It doesn't surprise me that it's on brother Ben's recommended reading list, though. After all, his other leisure-time activities include vandalizing classic cars."

Carrie frowned. "I'd rather not talk about that."

"You'd prefer to return to our earlier topic? That would be homicidal psychopaths. Makes brother Ben seem downright wholesome, doesn't it?"

Tyler took the book from her, glanced at the sinister cover and the blurb that promised "horrific terror and spine-chilling suspense." He threw the book into the trash can with a dramatic flourish. "I suggest you switch to romance novels, Carrie. There is a wallfull to choose from at any Tremaine bookstore. They won't keep you up at night."

"Sometimes they do," Carrie said frankly. "For entirely different reasons, though."

Tyler arched his brows. "Horniness rather than horrific terror?"

"But you're wide awake, just the same."

"Yeah, tell me about it." Tyler laughed shortly. "At this point, I think I'd prefer horrific terror. Maybe I should retrieve that book from the trash. The spine-chilling suspense might take my mind off... other things."

"Didn't your date cooperate tonight?" Carrie feigned sympathy that she did not feel, trying hard to ignore a piercing stab of jealousy.

Tyler removed his coat and draped it over the chair. He loosened his tie, unfastened the top buttons of his shirt and rolled up the sleeves to his elbows. Carrie watched him silently, trying to anticipate his next move, wondering how she could manage to stay cool and calm when her nerves were already in a heightened, jangled state.

"May I have something to drink?" he asked politely.

Carrie stared at him. As a highly anticipated next move, his request was ridiculously anticlimactic. "Of course. What would you like?"

"Anything as long as it's cold. I'm starting to dehydrate. It's about a hundred degrees in here tonight."

"I closed all the windows and bolted them," she admitted.

"Let me guess—the killer in the story gained entry through his victims' open windows."

Carrie nodded. "He took an open window as a sign that he was welcome to come in."

"Hmm, kind of like Dracula, but not as classy without the cape, fangs and alternative bat identity."

"It's not funny." Carrie shivered. "I'll never feel safe opening another window unless I live in a high-rise on the twentieth floor."

She poured Tyler a glass of lemonade loaded with ice cubes, then poured one for herself. They sat down at the kitchen table. "How did you know I had a date tonight?" he asked curiously.

"By what you're wearing. You look like prime date material."

"Somehow I don't think my date tonight would agree." He took a long drink of the lemonade. "Gwenda—that's the name of my unfortunate date—was quite solicitous at the end, however. She kindly pointed out that my *problem* was probably temporary and due to stress and that I shouldn't let it drive me to do anything foolish." He felt his sense of humor, temporarily obliterated by the night's events, beginning to return.

Carrie looked mystified. "What problem?"

"Gwenda supplied me with the number of a suicide hotline. Just in case," Tyler continued dryly. "She said she knows how hard men take such things. I know she meant well, but hard was not a particularly tactful choice of words."

Carrie's jaw dropped. "You mean you didn't...you couldn't..." She lifted her hand to her mouth.

"If you're smiling, I swear I'll pour the contents of this glass, including the ice cubes, down the back of your robe."

"I'm not smiling," Carrie said, trying to rearrange her lips so that she wasn't. "Gwenda's right, you know. We learned in nursing school that it's not uncommon for men to experience a temporary...that—uh—there are many different factors that might cause..."

"There is no problem, not with me," Tyler growled. "Come over here and see, if you don't believe me. Better yet, come over here and feel."

"I believe you," Carrie said quickly. "You've never displayed any evidence of a—a—problem around me."

"And that, *my friend,* is an entirely different problem with ramifications all its own. Why, for example, do you turn me on while I'm sitting here drinking sickeningly sweet lemonade in a stifling kitchen discussing serial killers while Gwenda—in a setting made for romance—completely turned me off?"

Carrie felt a warm glow spread through her. "Am I supposed to answer that or is it simply a rhetorical question?"

"What it is, is some sort of weird cosmic joke, and I think it's being played on me."

Carrie smiled at him, that incomparable smile of hers that lighted her face and made her blue eyes shine with jewel-like brilliance. Tyler gazed raptly at her. Her smiled seemed to touch his soul in some deep recess that had never before been reached.

They both looked away at the same time, breaking their gaze but not the warm, intangible bond that seemed to connect them.

"Is the lemonade really sickeningly sweet?" Carrie asked solicitously. "If you'd rather have something else—"

"Oh, I'd rather have something else, all right." Tyler stretched his legs full-length under the table and his knees touched hers.

Carrie did not move. She refused to behave like a skittish virgin, especially after he'd already caught her acting like a high-strung scaredy-cat, spooked by her own imagination.

"But you won't give me what I'd rather have," Tyler drawled. "Will you, Carrie?"

"Not unless it involves something liquid in a glass."

"I figured as much." Tyler drained the contents of his glass and stood up. "If I leave now, are you going to be able to get to sleep or are you going to lie in bed frozen with fear, listening for a maniac trying to jimmy your windows open?"

Carrie winced. She'd been doing exactly that until she couldn't stand it anymore and had gotten up and turned on all the lights, deciding that it was a perfect time to do all those household chores she hadn't had a chance to do during normal waking hours.

"Your face and your eyes are very expressive," Tyler said. "Or else my people-reading skills are particularly acute tonight. You'd like me to stay."

"Tyler, we've been through all this before." Carrie sighed. "I can't go to bed with you."

"Honey, you couldn't pay me to spend the night in that unair-conditioned sweatbox you call your bedroom. I'll bunk with the triplets in the only habitable room in the house. Just give me a pillow and I'll sleep on their floor."

"Oh, I couldn't possibly let you—"

He took her hand and dragged her from the kitchen, flicking off the light as they left the room. "It won't be a first. I've spent my share of nights sacked out on the old fraternity house floor during my college years. And heat bothers me much more than the lack of a mattress."

Though a fan oscillated valiantly, her bedroom was as intolerably stuffy as he'd expected. Tyler escorted her into it, staying just long enough to collect the quilt and pillow that she gave him. Sleuth, the big striped tabby, was sprawled across her bed and didn't stir when Carrie slipped between the sheets.

Another first, Tyler mused. This was certainly the night for them. The pleasure of his company in bed had been rejected in favor of a cat's. He slipped quietly into the nursery and spread the quilt on the floor. The room was blessedly cool and dark, except for the dim glow of a small star-shaped night-light plugged into the wall socket.

Before he lay down, Tyler walked to each crib and peered at the sleeping child within. Emily was on her tummy, all tangled up in a pink blanket, Dylan lay on his left side, his small arms wrapped around a rather bedraggled plush lamb, and Franklin was flat on his back, his thumb in his mouth. They looked so small, so innocent. Three babies, helpless and dependent. And the one all three depended on was their mother, their only parent. Carrie.

Tyler closed his eyes and visualized Carrie in her own bed, just a door away. She looked too young to be the mother of three children; she was small and soft, and when she batted those big blue eyes of hers, she looked as innocent as her little daughter. But Carrie was not helpless or dependent.

Quite the contrary. The lady could take care of herself and her own, she'd made that quite clear.

So what was he doing here, sacked out on the nursery floor, while she cuddled with her cat in the room next door? Carrie hadn't asked him to stay but he knew that she'd wanted him to. She had allowed herself to depend on him. Tonight, she had needed him. And what, he mused, had he found so irresistibly appealing about that?

He thought about it as he stripped to his boxer shorts, tossing his clothes onto the small plastic chair near the wall. People often wanted and needed things, both tangible and intangible, from him because he was Tyler Tremaine and he had all the trappings and influence and power of the Tremaine name and wealth behind him.

In his personal life, the same held true. Women wanted to be seen with him because of who he was and where he could take them, for the entries he could provide. He knew he had a handsome face and a good body; he'd also been complimented on his charm. But he never kidded himself about the power of the name Tremaine. With it, he could look like a troll and have the personality of a fanatical terrorist, but his popularity wouldn't suffer a bit.

But he couldn't remember anyone ever wanting him, just him. Tyler, shorn of the Tremaine and all that his surname entailed. Not until tonight.

Being here tonight had nothing to do with being a Tremaine. Tonight he was simply a man whose presence ensured a young mother peace of mind against the demons that her idiot brother's choice of reading material had inspired. Tonight, the act of *being* was enough. He wasn't wanted or needed for favors, deals, sex or money. It was enough that he was simply here, lying on the floor. Just being.

Through the years, he had passed through many different stages and phases; Tyler vaguely recalled some of them as he stared at the three cribs surrounding him. He decided this current phase of his was the most inexplicable and unfathomable by far. And he fervently hoped it was a very temporary one.

"Uh-oh!"

The syllables, loud and distinct, penetrated Tyler's consciousness, jerking him awake. He opened his eyes just in time to see a blue toy pig flying out of the crib to his left.

"Uh-oh!" Franklin called again. The toddler was standing up in his crib, beaming down at Tyler. Having hurled the pig, he tossed out a bright red teddy bear.

Tyler sat up. "Good morning to you, too." He tossed the pig and the bear back into Franklin's crib. The little boy laughed heartily and threw them back, along with every other stuffed occupant of his crib. There seemed to be an astonishing number of them. Tyler kept throwing the stuffed animals back until he realized that this was a game with no signs of ending.

By this time, Franklin's boisterous laughter had awakened Dylan and Emily. They both stood in their respective cribs, watching the fun. When the green lamb came sailing out of Dylan's crib, Tyler realized that unless he called an immediate halt, he was going to be inundated with every single toy the triplets could get their busy little hands on.

"Okay, okay, that's enough." He stood up and then groaned as his body protested the too-short night's sleep on the too-hard floor. It had been a long, long time since those nights on the fraternity-house floor. He was stiff, he ached and he was facing three energetic, bright-eyed little tykes who'd begun jumping up and down in their cribs, shrieking "up" and "go."

He looked expectantly at the door, waiting for Carrie to come through it. She didn't, but the babies' demands to be sprung from their cribs vocally increased. Tyler made an executive decision, though he was more unsure of this one than any he'd ever sent down at Tremaine Incorporated.

"Okay, I'll get you guys out," he said hesitantly. He lifted Emily out of the crib. Her little pajamas felt rather soggy. Her brothers' pj's were similarly damp. Tyler momentarily panicked. "Look, kids, I'm sorry, but I just don't do diapers!"

The children didn't seem to care. They raced out of the room, and Tyler started to follow them, then paused to glance into Carrie's bedroom. She was sound asleep, curled on her side in the middle of the bed, the sheet pulled up to her chin.

She looked young and angelic. Tyler's heart stirred, then a flash of sensual heat seared him. She looked sexy and desirable, too. The combination seemed paradoxical—sexy *and* angelic?—but Carrie embodied it.

He didn't have time to ponder the puzzle. The triplets were heading down the stairs. Dylan and Franklin sensibly sat down and moved from stair to stair on their bottoms. Emily, however, started down on foot, and her balance struck Tyler as alarmingly precarious. He scooped her up in his arms, while she was wobbling at the edge of one stair. Looking down, the staircase seemed impossibly steep. He visualized her tumbling down and landing in a heap at the bottom, and his arms tightened more firmly around her.

Then he noticed the safety gate unlocked and pushed aside. He vaguely recalled Carrie lingering briefly in the hall last night to fasten it. How had the children managed to unlock it?

"I can see where the three of you working together as a gang have it all over kids your age who are born singly," he remarked. Their reply required a translation and there was no interpreter there to supply it, but Tyler was certain he was right. You couldn't take your eyes off these three, not even to gaze lustfully at their mother for a few moments.

He fared better in the kitchen, putting a bib on each child before strapping them into the high chairs, just as he'd seen Carrie do. They were extremely cheerful, grinning and babbling in that Pidgin English they spoke. They seemed glad he was there, glad they were out of their cribs and in their chairs. Their company was uncomplicated and upbeat. Tyler found himself smiling and conversing with them, though the conversation was admittedly on parallel tracks.

Feeling more relaxed and confident with them, he set about making breakfast. It seemed the obvious thing to do. He poured Cheerios and milk in three plastic bowls, then gave one to each child, along with a spoon and a napkin.

Emily made an attempt to dip the spoon into the bowl, but had no luck capturing any Cheerios. The milk in the spoon spilled out when she turned it upside down on its way to her mouth.

Dylan didn't bother at all with the spoon, immediately tossing it to the floor and digging into his cereal bowl with both hands. The milk sloshed over the sides of the bowl and he splashed in it a bit. Franklin was more interested in the napkin. He ignored the cereal, milk and spoon while he investigated the strange piece of paper he'd been given, even ripping off a corner to taste it.

The cat appeared in the kitchen, glared balefully at Tyler and issued an imperious meow. "I know, I know," Tyler said, recognizing critcism when he heard it. "I should have served the cereal and the milk separately. And the napkins were a major mistake." He watched Emily stuff hers into the bowl, then remove it, studying it curiously before submerging it again.

Sleuth jumped up onto the counter and meowed again. All three children grew wildly excited at the sight of the cat. "Key, Key," cried Emily in a not-too-bad attempt at "Kitty." Dylan made a sound similar to a meow and Sleuth meowed right back at him, twice as loud.

Carrie entered the kitchen at that moment and stared at Tyler, who was wearing his boxer shorts and gazing bemusedly from the babies in their high chairs to the howling cat on the counter.

"You look like you just found yourself transported into the Twilight Zone," she said, flustered. She'd awakened with a start and rushed into the nursery, only to find the cribs empty. Without bothering to pull on a robe, she'd dashed to the kitchen, and now Tyler's gaze was focused intently on her.

"Everything's cool," he said lightly. He deftly snatched the three mangled, soaked napkins away from the high-chair trays and threw them into the trash, where they landed on the dark design of the serial killer book jacket. "The kids and I were getting along great, but that cat hates me," he added.

"He's hungry. I'll give him his breakfast." Carrie reached for a can of cat food, and Sleuth wound his way between her ankles, purring loudly.

Tyler watched her. Last night he'd wondered what she had on under her robe. Now he knew—a short, white cotton nightgown, the collar and cuffs edged with white eyelet, midthigh in length, loosely cut and modestly demure.

He sank down onto one of the kitchen chairs. He knew he was in big trouble when the sight of a woman in such a decidedly chaste garment struck him as alluring and erotic to the point where he felt weak-kneed with desire.

"Tyler, thanks so much for staying last night," Carrie said softly, coming to stand beside his chair. She laid her hand on his bare shoulder, feeling the warmth of his skin and hard muscle beneath her fingers. "I fell asleep right away."

"No nightmares about bloodthirsty creeps?" Tyler asked huskily.

"Not even one. And thanks for getting the kids up this morning and giving them breakfast. I can't believe I slept so late."

"Carrie, it's 7:00 a.m. That's hardly what I'd call sleeping in late."

"But I usually hear them the minute they wake up. I don't know how I slept through it this morning." Had some subconscious part of her mind realized that Tyler was there and would take over for her?

Tyler wondered the same thing and felt ridiculously flattered. "I didn't mind," he mumbled. "But I drew the line at diaper detail."

Carrie smiled. "I don't blame you." Trembling slightly, her fingers drifted down his arm, then back again, and she moved closer to his chair until her body was touching him. Her face was flushed, her heart pounding. She knew exactly what she was doing and knew she shouldn't be doing it. But she couldn't seem to make herself stop. She wanted to touch him, desperately. She wanted to arouse him.

Tyler responded at once, pulling her onto his lap with lightning speed. "That move worked so well the other night, I thought I'd try it again," he said with a husky laugh.

"You ought to make it a permanent part of your repertoire," Carrie advised.

Tyler thought of the dating-mating rituals he'd all but standardized over the years and suddenly the entire process seemed silly and irrelevant. How long had it been since he'd actually enjoyed it all—the meeting, the chase, the inevitable surrender? Last night's scene with Gwenda certainly pointed to a case of social, sexual burnout.

"My repertoire, such as it was, seems to have gone the way of the dial telephone and black-and-white television and the vinyl LP," he said dryly. In fact the entire concept of the carefree bachelor playboy struck him as obsolete and déclassé, a cliché that had become its own caricature.

"Your confidence is shaken because of what happened or didn't happen last night with—what was her name?—Griselda?" Carrie suggested sweetly.

Tyler caught the underlying snide note in her voice and smiled. "Her name is Gwenda," he supplied helpfully.

"Of course, Gwenda." Carrie decided she hated the name. It was right up there with Rhandee. She shifted slightly, and in doing so rotated her bottom against the hair-roughened muscular columns of his thighs. She was extremely aware of his lack of attire and she savored the feel of his hard strength beneath her. Pressing her torso lightly against his, the soft weight of her breasts rubbed his broad, bare chest. She felt his swift masculine response, and a pulsing heat surged through her.

"Maybe I should call Gwenda with the good news that my problem was very temporary. That I won't be needing that hot line, after all." Tyler caught Carrie's hands, which were toying with the wiry tufts of hair on his chest. Though he'd stilled her hands, she moved her body lightly, sinuously against him.

He groaned, firm and full and yearning to succumb to the temptation she presented. "Sweet, innocent little Carrie," he gritted. "Do you have any idea what you're doing to me?"

Carrie blushed. Oh, she knew. In fact, the idea was all her own. She was not so sweet and innocent. In fact, there were names for women who did what she was doing; she'd heard them. But not until her path had crossed Tyler Tremaine's could she ever have been accused of acting like one.

"I'm not teasing you," she blurted out, protesting her thoughts aloud. After all, teasing implied some calculated control over her actions, and she had none. She wanted to arouse him, to make him respond to her, so much so that she couldn't *not* do it.

"Oh yes, you are, baby," Tyler countered. "You most certainly are." He curved his hand around the nape of her neck and pulled her head down to nestle in the hollow of his chest. "The question is 'Why?' " His fingers began a slow, sensuous massage of her neck.

Carrie felt herself going limp against him, while the warmth in her belly grew hotter and sharper, sending shards of pleasure all through her.

"Why, Carrie?" Tyler nuzzled her ear, his teeth toying with the soft lobe, before nibbling a trail of small kisses along the smooth, graceful length of her neck. "Do you get your kicks turning me on so you can have the pleasure of stopping me cold?"

His words had the effect of dousing her with a bucket of ice water. "No!" Carrie cried, so vehemently that the triplets ceased their breakfast experimentations and looked over at her. She jumped to her feet as if she'd been mechanically propelled off his lap.

"No, no, no!" Emily echoed, her tone laced with disapproval.

"No!" roared Dylan defiantly.

Franklin, who had just dunked his face into his bowl of milk, burst into tears.

"He thinks we're scolding him," Carrie said and rushed to comfort her small son.

Tyler grimaced. He didn't want to let Carrie go, he didn't want to end what could have been an interesting, revealing conversation. His body was taut and throbbing. He wanted... It was very obvious what he wanted and just as obvious that he wasn't going to get it. Not with three toddlers looking on, one of them sobbing, the other two growing increasingly restless.

Tyler stood up, sighing. He was already exhausted and emotionally spent and it was not yet seven-thirty in the morning. He decided later that his weakened mental and physical state had played a definite role in the invitation he impulsively issued to Carrie. "Do you and the mighty mites want to swim in my pool later today, when I get home from work?"

Carrie turned around, Franklin in her arms. He had ceased wailing and was chomping happily on a biscuit she'd given him. "Are you having another party tonight?"

They both remembered that it had been one week ago today that he had invited her and the children to his last party and that his motives had been decidedly sinister. Tyler's green eyes met her wary blue ones for a long moment.

"No, there's no party," he said quietly. "It'll just be the—" he paused to count "—the five of us."

Say no, Carrie, she ordered herself. *You can't keep your hands off the man when you're near him, and he knows it. When and if he decides to turn up the heat, you'll melt like a snowflake in the sun. And how will you reconcile that with your undying love for Ian?*

She chewed her lip nervously. "I really don't think that—"

"I have life jackets the kids can wear," Tyler assured her. "When they're strapped into them, they won't be able to slip under the water, so the two of us should be able to manage the three of them, even in the deeper water."

She hadn't given a thought to life jackets for the children to wear in the pool! But Tyler had. Carrie was horrified that her own thoughts had been on sex, not water safety. Caught off balance and off guard, she heard herself stammer, "Okay—we'll come over."

"I'll give you a call when I get home, probably around six. Maybe a little earlier." Tyler laid one hand on Emily's small blond head, the other on Dylan's. "I'd better get myself dressed and out of here. I have a meeting downtown in less than an hour."

The meeting went smoothly, with the outcome favorable to Tremaine Incorporated, as expected. Tyler and his brother Cole emerged from the building into midmorning city heat.

"This weekend is supposed to be another scorcher," Cole remarked. "I guess you're heading to the beach to escape the heat and party till you—"

"No, I'm not going to the beach this weekend," Tyler cut in. At his older brother's look of surprise, he added quickly, "I, uh, have plans here at home. In the city."

"What's her name?" Cole chuckled.

Tyler gave his brother a good-natured, wouldn't-you-like-to-know sock in the arm. He had no intention of letting his brother in on this strange relationship—Lord, he hated that word and all the baggage it implied!—he and Carrie seemed to have developed. And it wasn't really a *relationship,* anyway, Tyler consoled himself. No, it couldn't be. Tyler Tremaine and a mother of three children? Who happened to be toddler triplets! Cole would find the notion as unbelievable as Tyler himself did.

"Hey, Cole, where did your kids get those orange life jackets they wear at the beach and on the boat?" Tyler asked.

"What?" Cole obviously considered the question a stunning non sequitur. He gaped at his younger brother.

"Those things would work in a pool, too, wouldn't they?" Tyler persisted.

"If you mean, would they keep a child afloat, the answer is yes," Cole replied carefully.

"Good. So where do you buy them?"

Staring strangely at him, Cole mentioned the names of several places.

"Thanks!" Tyler clapped his brother on the back. "And in case I don't see you back at the office later, have a good weekend."

"Thank you, I will." Cole continued to eye his brother. "Chelsea and I are planning to take Daniel and the baby to the beach this weekend."

Tyler imagined the triplets playing in the sand and running into the waves at the water's edge. He grinned.

''They'll have a great time. Probably try to eat the sand, though.'' If they were willing to sample paper napkins, they would undoubtedly try to snack on sand.

Cole was completely taken aback. ''What? No expounding on the hell of traveling with small children? What about your theory that it's stupid to take little kids anywhere because they never know where they are, anyway?''

''You just have to persevere, brother. Kids are a lot smarter than people give them credit for.'' With that, Tyler headed toward the parking garage, leaving his wide-eyed brother standing speechless on the sidewalk.

Eight

"**O**kay—ready, set, go!" called Tyler.

An excited, grinning Dylan jumped into the pool. His head bobbed above the water and he kicked his little legs, splashing and shrieking with delight, being kept safely afloat by his bright orange life jacket.

Tyler ferried him through the water to the part of the pool where Carrie was pulling Emily and Franklin around in a blow-up plastic boat.

Dylan began to flail his arms and legs wildly. "Go!" he demanded. "Go, go!"

Tyler groaned. The little boy had been jumping into the pool for the past twenty minutes. "He *can't* want to do it again! He's already made at least a hundred-fifty jumps. And that's a conservative estimate."

Carrie sensed his endurance waning. "Why don't you give Emily and Franklin a boat ride and I'll catch Dylan when he jumps in," she suggested.

"Lady, you've got a deal," Tyler said gratefully.

It was nearly eight o'clock, well past the children's bed-time, and they were having their second swim of the day. He'd fetched them at five-thirty and brought them all over to the pool to swim for an hour, then ordered Chinese food for everybody, which they'd eaten back at Carrie's place. He'd been amused at the triplets' introduction to sweet-and-sour chicken, a dish they had heartily, if messily, consumed right down to the last piece of sauce-drenched pineapple. In an expansive, indulgent mood, he had suggested a return to the pool, and Carrie had immediately agreed.

It was a far different scene in and around the pool this Friday than it had been this time last week. Tyler looked at the plethora of toys floating in the water, all of which he had purchased earlier that day, along with the orange life jackets the children wore. An old song, "If My Friends Could See Me Now" played mockingly in his head.

He blocked it out and trained his eyes on Carrie, who was standing in the shallow water, waiting for Dylan to complete his one-hundred-seventy-ninth jump. She was wearing her yellow-and-white polka dot swimsuit, and his gaze lingered on the creamy bare skin of her midriff. Moving closer, he could clearly see the enticing thrust of her nipples against the wet, clinging fabric of her swimsuit.

He imagined himself lowering the bra of her suit and looking at her, touching her, putting his mouth on those sensitive little peaks. Tyler felt his body stir. To distract himself, he dove under the water and resurfaced behind the boat. Emily and Franklin laughed. They thought he was playing some aquatic version of peekaboo. Fortunately, they were too young and innocent to know that he was caught in the throes of lust for their sweet, devoted mother.

"Speedboat ride," he called out, a little desperately. He pulled the boat through the water, back and forth, faster and faster, the children crowing with delight. The exercise was a very effective antidote for lust.

"Shall we do this again tomorrow?" he asked Carrie half an hour later, as they hauled the three crying babies across the yard toward her house. The children had been incensed at being taken out of the water. All three had screamed at the top of their lungs in protest—and kept howling, all the way home.

Tyler was oddly flattered. He interpreted their reaction as the toddlers' way of saying they'd had the time of their young lives.

Carrie was amazed that he'd invited them again. She had watched him playing with the kids in the water all evening, without a single break from them. When the triple tantrum had begun, she'd expected him to flee gratefully, not issue a repeat invitation.

Her eyes were drawn to Tyler's shoulders and chest, wet and sleek with water, the dark hair matted to his skin. He held Franklin and Dylan in his strong arms, and they looked small and safe there, clinging to Tyler exhaustedly while wailing that the fun had to end. A bittersweet pang assailed her.

They carried the children inside the house and up to their room. "You haven't given me an answer, you know." Tyler pressed, setting the two little boys down. "What about swimming tomorrow?"

"You know they'd love to." Carrie knelt to dry all three wet, squirming toddlers. "But do you really want to—"

"Do *you* want to?" he cut in, leaning against the wall, watching her. She moved as quickly as the children, her every motion competent and efficient.

"Yes," she admitted softly. She tackled Dylan and stuffed him into his pajamas while Emily and Franklin, giggling now, threw themselves on the big stuffed panda in the corner of the room. She would have them all dressed and in bed in under ten minutes and then she and Tyler would be alone. . . .

"Okay. We'll swim after their afternoon nap tomorrow," Tyler said decisively, walking out the door. "See you then. 'Night kids," he called.

Carrie felt a hot rush of tears sting her eyes. They pooled there, burning but not falling, while she put the babies into their cribs, while she showered and washed her hair. Tyler hadn't stayed, and who could blame him for leaving?

"Do you get your kicks turning me on so you can have the pleasure of stopping me cold?" he'd asked. He thought she was a tease. Carrie thought of the wild desire and hot pleasure his kisses and caresses evoked, and she shuddered with need. No, there was absolutely no pleasure in stopping what she was coming to want more and more.

But what if she didn't stop him? What if she were to cast aside all caution and control and make love with Tyler? It was an out-of-character question about an equally out-of-character act. She'd never been one to casually indulge in sex for sex's sake. Her only lover had been Ian Wilcox, and they'd waited until their wedding night to make love for the first time because she'd wanted to be a virgin bride.

But she wasn't a virgin anymore, and Tyler wasn't the easy-to-please, placid man Ian had been. Tyler was demanding and impulsive, aggressive and confident. And sexy. She thought of his intense, green-eyed gaze, of the way he touched her, kissed her. A hot twist of excitement unwound deep inside her and the sudden acceleration of her pulses left her breathless.

Call him! urged a wild little voice inside her head. Firmly, swiftly, Carrie stifled the impulse with a harsh reality check. She was not going to have her heart broken, like poor Alexa who had confused a man's desire with a man's love. She was not going to be hurt by another loss in her life. She had her children, she had her work. She was *not* going to have Tyler Tremaine, and the sooner she stopped wanting him . . .

Carrie gulped back the unexpected sob that rose in her throat. She had to stop wanting him!

* * *

Tyler held a wailing Emily in his arms as he stood in the doorway and watched Carrie, dressed in her white nurse's uniform, drive away from the house. Alexa was trying to comfort an equally distraught Franklin and Dylan.

"Mommy!" shrieked Emily, as if her heart was breaking. Tyler felt a searing pang of empathy. He knew from firsthand experience how it felt to be a young child, crying for a mother who wasn't there.

"It's a damn shame Carrie has to leave these children every weekend," he said fiercely, speaking his thoughts aloud. "They're babies—they need their mother. They shouldn't have to be without her."

"I know," Alexa said quietly. "I think so, too."

Tyler looked at her in surprise. He hadn't expected Carrie's sister to agree with anything he had to say. Alexa had been coolly aloof toward him since she'd arrived a half hour ago to find him eating hot dogs in the backyard with Carrie and the triplets. She'd barely said a word when Carrie told her about their earlier afternoon swim in Tyler's pool, but it didn't take his much-vaunted assessing skills to divine Alexa's wary disapproval.

He'd stuck around, probably because Carrie and Alexa expected him to leave and he did not want to be so predictable. He hadn't counted on the triplets' harrowing reaction to Carrie's departure for the hospital. They'd burst into tears when they saw her in her uniform and frantically clung to her, despite her attempts to comfort them. Finally, Tyler and Alexa had to pry the three loose so Carrie could get out the door. Tyler was still disturbed. It was terrible to have to wrench small children from their mother. It wasn't fair, it wasn't right!

"Let's have some ice cream!" Alexa said in an overly loud, overly cheerful voice. "Come on, let's go into the kitchen and have ice cream, right now!"

She led the still-sniffling Dylan and Franklin away from the door toward the kitchen. From her perch in his arms,

Emily looked Tyler directly in the eye. "I keem?" she asked.
A shuddering sob shook her little body, and she lay her head
down on Tyler's shoulder.

Tyler hugged her tight. "Emily, Mommy will be back
soon, I promise. And tomorrow we'll go swimming again.
We'll ride in your boat, too. Now, let's go get some ice
cream before those brothers of yours eat it all up." He kept
up a running commentary as he carried her into the kitchen.

Instead of putting her in the high chair, he held the little
girl on his lap while she ate her ice cream. He chatted to
Dylan and Franklin as they sat in their chairs, shoveling ice
cream into their mouths. He noted with interest that all three
used their spoons far more effectively with the ice cream
than with yesterday's cereal and milk. He filed away the fact
for future reference.

"Looks like the ice cream did the trick," Tyler remarked. "Nobody's crying anymore."

Alexa, sitting across the table from him, actually smiled.
"I know it's probably wrong, but I bribe them with ice
cream or cookies every time Carrie leaves. I hate to see them
cry. I hope they get over their separation anxiety before I
turn them into blimps!"

"That'll never happen. Not the way this trio expends energy." Tyler retrieved a blob of vanilla ice cream that Emily
accidentally dropped on his shirt. "You watch the kids for
both shifts, every single weekend Carrie works?"

Alexa nodded.

For the first time, Tyler truly appreciated all that that
entailed. "That's extremely generous of you," he said
thoughtfully.

Alexa shrugged. "I'd do anything to help Carrie and the
babies."

"But it's quite a sacrifice for you to make, giving up every
weekend to baby-sit. What if you have . . . plans?"

"You mean, like a date? No problem. I've retired from
dating," Alexa replied succinctly.

Tyler laughed. "Oh, come on! You're too young to say that. And way too pretty to have no social life. You're—"

"You sound like my mother," Alexa said dryly. "Why is it so hard to believe that I'd rather spend my weekends with my adorable niece and nephews than to pursue the *dating scene?*" She made it sound akin to food poisoning.

Tyler's brows narrowed. "Does your premature retirement from dating have something to do with Ryan Cassidy?"

Alexa froze. "I don't want to talk about him. Not now or ever."

The wounds inflicted by Cassidy hadn't yet healed, Tyler concluded. He wondered what had happened between them and how long ago. Could brother Ben's atrocious deed have been justifiable? But he knew by looking into Alexa's haunted blue eyes that this was not a subject to be pursued.

"How long has Carrie been working those back-to-back killer shifts?" he asked instead.

Alexa visibly relaxed. "She went back to work shortly after the triplets' first birthday. Mom and I didn't want her to, but Dad told her she ought to get back out into the world, that she needed the confidence that comes with being able to support herself and her family."

"That sounds awfully harsh to me," Tyler remarked, frowning his disapproval.

"Not harsh," countered Alexa. "Tough. Practical. That's Daddy. He's a colonel in the air force and his motto is 'When the going gets tough, the tough get going.' Dad genuinely wanted to help Carrie cope."

"Then why didn't he and your mother help her with the triplets?"

"They did," Alexa said. "She went to live with them right after Ian was killed, while she was still pregnant. She and the babies lived with them until three months ago, when Dad got orders to go overseas to Germany. Carrie didn't want to go with them, and she'd inherited this place from Ian's uncle, so she decided to move in here. She says Daddy was right about her working, that she really did start to feel more confident and independent. But I know how hard this schedule is on her. Since I work all week—I'm a physical therapist at the Hospital Center—Carrie takes care of the triplets without help from anyone, and she does a wonderful job of it. I think it's the babies and the passage of time that's helped her cope with Ian's loss.''

"Do you think that she—''

"You're interested in my sister, aren't you?'' Alexa interrupted. "Don't bother to deny it. I've seen the way you look at her.''

"We're friends,'' Tyler said cautiously.

"I've seen some of your friends, last week at that party of yours.'' Alexa eyed him sternly. "I'm warning you now—don't even think of including my sister in that group.''

And Tyler, who didn't take kindly to being lectured or threatened, and usually retaliated in kind, merely replied, "You're very loyal to your sister. But you don't have to worry about Carrie. I'm currently on sabbatical from the dating and party scene myself.''

He hadn't considered such an option until now, but it suddenly seemed an excellent idea. He could use a break from his social life which had inexplicably become tedious rather than fun.

"Well, time for me to go,'' he said, glancing at his watch.

Emily dropped her spoon and it clattered to the floor. "No go!'' she exclaimed, screwing up her face to cry again. "No, no go.''

Alexa had freed Dylan and Franklin from their high chairs, and they watched their sister cling to Tyler. Suddenly Dylan crawled under the table, bellowing "No!'' and Franklin began to cry.

"They don't want you to go,'' Alexa said, astonished. She stared from the toddlers to Tyler. "They really like you.'' She sounded flabbergasted at the notion.

Tyler didn't hold it against her. His popularity with Carrie's children would mystify his own family as well since he rarely paid the slightest attention to the youngest generation of Tremaines. But Dylan, Emily and Franklin were different from any other children he'd ever met. They were cuter. Funnier. More interesting. He couldn't explain why, but they just were.

"I'll stay until they're in bed," he offered. Granted, it was an unorthodox way for him to spend a Saturday night, but the evening was still young; he'd have plenty of time to do something later. And he couldn't bring himself to disappoint his little fan club.

"So he stayed and helped you put the kids to bed?" Carrie repeated incredulously. She'd arrived home from the hospital an hour ago and was sipping iced tea in the backyard with Alexa while watching the triplets play.

Alexa nodded. "Then he left. He seems to genuinely like the kids, Carrie. They're certainly crazy about him. What's been going on around here, anyway?"

"I don't know," Carrie murmured. She rubbed her temples with her fingers. She'd been awake for over twenty-four hours straight and was feeling the peculiar disorienting effects of sleep deprivation. The children were always awake by the time she got home in the morning and wanted her attention. She couldn't rush off to her bedroom and sleep without spending some time with them first.

"Tyler says he's taken a sabbatical from dating," Alexa said, glancing sidelong at her sister. "I wonder why."

"Who knows?" Carrie shrugged. Did his unsatisfactory evening with Gwenda have anything to do with it? Whatever his reason, one thing was very clear—if Tyler wasn't dating, he wasn't pursuing other women. Carrie felt a surge of glee, though she deliberately concealed it from her sister.

"I guess it does explain why he's been coming around here, though," mused Alexa. "Spending time with the triplets is about as far from dating as one could possibly get."

Carrie felt deflated. "That's true," she admitted.

"But you're here, too." Alexa stared at her sister. "When he's here, he is spending time with you as well as the kids. That could mean—"

"We—Tyler and I—are just friends, Alexa."

"Mmm-hmm. That's what he said."

"Ty, Ty, Ty!" The children's voices rose into a chorus of delighted shrieks and squeals, drawing Carrie's and Alexa's attention to the hedge, where Tyler had appeared. He was wearing a pair of comfortably baggy shorts and a loose-fitting white shirt.

"I thought I heard the posse at play back here," he said, stopping to scoop up all three children in his arms. He was ridiculously pleased they'd remembered his name, which they seemed to have picked up all on their own yesterday.

He started across the yard toward Carrie but she met him in the middle of it.

The mere sight of him made her restless and edgy—hot, even. And not from the eighty-plus degrees already registering on the thermometer.

"Looks like you—uh—captured the whole posse single-handedly," she said huskily.

"Do I get a reward?" His tone was suggestive, his green eyes glittering.

Carrie felt a flush of heat suffuse her. She felt soft and weak and half-dizzy from fatigue. Hardly an ideal state; she needed to be at the peak of her wits to deal with Tyler.

"Where's your snappy comeback?" Tyler demanded. "You're rarely without one."

"Well, this is one of those rare times. I'm temporarily out of quips."

"You look exhausted," Tyler said bluntly. But the dark violet circles under her eyes gave her an aura of fragility, somehow heightening her appeal. He wondered if there were *any* circumstances where he wouldn't find her desirable.

"We had a wild night last night," she told him. "Four deliveries, including a set of twins and two first-time mothers in their forties."

Tyler shuddered. "Kindly spare me the gynecological horror stories." The triplets began to squirm, and he obligingly set them on their feet. They wandered off toward their makeshift sandpile in the corner of the yard.

"I came over to tell you that a truck is parked in front of your house and a couple guys are heading to your front door. Looks like they're making a delivery," he added.

"That can't be," Carrie said. At the same moment, Alexa called, "Carrie, someone's ringing the bell. Want me to answer it or stay here with the kids?"

"I'll get it," Carrie replied, going through the house to the front door. Tyler followed her. "There must be some mistake. I haven't ordered anything."

Two deliverymen stood on her front porch with a large box between them. "Bring it on in," Tyler ordered. "Take it upstairs, second room on the right."

"But—what—?" Carrie spluttered. Tyler fastened his hands around her shoulders and maneuvered her aside, out of the men's way. "Tyler, I didn't buy anything!"

"No, but I did. That's your air conditioner. They're going to install it in your bedroom window. There's a bigger model they'll install next in the living room. It has enough BTUs to cool the entire downstairs."

Carrie gaped at him. It took a full minute to regain her power of speech, but she finally managed to gasp, "You bought me an air conditioner?"

"Two of them. Room-sized window units."

"But you can't do that!"

"Why can't I? It doesn't look like brother Ben is going to come through with that secondhand deal you mentioned, and we're in the middle of a heat wave." He started toward the stairs. "I'm going to go up and make sure they're in—"

"Tyler, wait." Carrie grabbed his arm with both hands, halting him. "It's very generous of you, but I—I can't accept air conditioners from you!"

"Why not? An air conditioner is hardly a personal, intimate gift like lingerie. Something like that would imply—well, you know what lingerie implies. But what's an air conditioner between friends?"

"Tyler, people do not go around giving other people air conditioners! It—it just isn't done!"

He shrugged lazily. "Maybe I'll start a new trend. I've always been on the cutting edge." He glanced down at her hands, which were clutching his arm. "Are you going to let go or am I going to drag you along with me?"

Carrie hung on to him. "Tyler, why are you doing this?"

He was silent for a moment, then raised his hands to cup her face between them. His eyes met hers and they stared at each other, tension shimmering between them. "Why don't you tell me, Carrie?" he growled. "Then we'll both know."

With that, he lowered his mouth to hers in a hard, hungry kiss that robbed her of her breath and the few wits she had left. Her lips parted instantly on impact and his tongue thrust deep into the moist hollow of her mouth. Her legs felt rubbery and unsteady, and she had to cling to him for support. Tyler supplied it by wrapping her in his arms, so close and so tight that she could feel the hard stirring of his flesh and the churning response of her own.

A responsive moan escaped from her throat and she pressed closer, feeling almost drunk as she clung to him. She felt the heat in her thighs, in her belly and breasts, burning and tingling along her every nerve. With a shuddering sigh, she melted against him in sweet, abject surrender.

Just as suddenly, his lips left hers and his arms fell away from her. Carrie wanted to cry out in protest. Swaying dizzily, her eyes flew open and she gazed up at Tyler to see him looking at her children, who had just burst noisily onto the scene with their aunt Alexa right behind them.

"Oh, don't mind us," Alexa said rather trenchantly. "You two friends just go on being friendly. The kids and I are headed upstairs to—"

"Alexa, I—we..." Flustered, flushed, Carrie let her voice trail off. She ran her hand through her hair, tousling it even more than Tyler had. "Tyler bought me an air conditioner. T—two of them."

Alexa raised her brows. "Well, wasn't that a friendly thing to do?"

"They needed it," Tyler said briskly. "After all, the pollen count and pollution index are at record highs and air conditioners are the first line of defense against allergies and asthma and—"

"Except none of us suffers from them," Carrie cut in. "Tyler, I really can't accept—"

"You can and you are," Tyler said flatly. "I'm going to give it to you and you're going to take it. Do you understand?"

His eyes seemed to bore into her, piercing her right to the core. Carrie swallowed hard, blushing, wondering what she could say, what she should do. She thought there was an underlying sexual connotation to his words, but maybe it was just her own fevered perceptions. When Tyler was around, her mind was clouded with sexual thoughts, references, deeds and needs....

She sat down on the bottom step and reached out to catch one of the babies. She nabbed Dylan, lifted him onto her lap and tried to cuddle him.

"You look ready to keel over." Tyler's voice sounded above her head. "As soon as both units are installed, Alexa and I are taking the kids to my pool to swim and you're going to your room to get some sleep, Carrie.''

"I'm impressed, Tyler. You bark out orders just like Dad, and you're not even in the military," Alexa said dryly.

"In the civilian business world, we call it 'making executive decisions.' And just like in the military, we in command expect to be obeyed." Tyler slipped his hands under Carrie's arms and effortlessly lifted her to her feet.

She clutched her small son, as her gaze locked with Tyler's. Her pupils were dilated, her heart was throbbing, her womb contracting with the memory of their hot kiss. Oh, how she wanted him. And she knew instinctively that the intensity of her passion transcended mere sexual desire. She was so very close to falling in love with the man...if she wasn't already in love with him.

Carrie dropped her eyes, not wanting Tyler to read too much there. She felt like she was sailing into a wild, uncharted sea without direction, and when she tried to think of Ian, to steady her, to calm and guide her, Tyler's presence filled her mind and her senses, blocking out anyone and anything else.

"I dropped over to see if I could help with the kids," Ben said later that evening as he strolled jauntily into Carrie's living room where Alexa sat alone, reading. He screeched to an abrupt halt and did an unconsciously comic double take at the sight of the air conditioner humming in the window. "I *thought* it felt cooler in here!" he exclaimed. "I didn't feel like I was suffocating the minute I walked in the door."

Alexa put down her book and stood up. "The babies are in bed for the night, so you're a little late to help," she informed him. "And the air conditioner—there are two of them actually, this one and one in Carrie's room—are compliments of Tyler Tremaine."

Ben was incredulous. "He air-conditioned Carrie's house?''

"Right neighborly of him, wasn't it?" drawled Alexa.

"I'll say! And it saves me from telling Carrie that I couldn't get her that secondhand unit for her bedroom." Ben sank down onto the sofa and sighed appreciatively. "It's so cool and comfortable in here now. Coming over here is going to be—Alexa, that's it!" He jumped to his feet, his blue eyes wide. "That's why he did it!"

"Could you be a little more specific, Ben? That's why who did what?"

"Tyler Tremaine hates the heat, and this place was megahot, so he set about changing things to suit himself. Why? Because he intends on spending a lot of time here this summer. A lot of time with Carrie, Alexa." Ben thrust his fist into the air in a gesture of victory. "Yes! She did it! She's got him hooked! A Tremaine! Do you know what this means, Alexa?"

Alexa stared at him impassively. "I can guess what you think it means for *you*, Ben. An office in the Tremaine Building with your name engraved on the door, your own personalized stationery and a fat expense account. Well, here's a word of advice—don't quit your current job just yet. So far, neither Carrie nor Tyler will admit to being anything more than friends."

Ben was undaunted. "It doesn't matter what they're saying, it can only mean that he's fallen hard for her. And the fact that Carrie accepted it means she's fallen for him, too."

"She really had no choice but to keep the air conditioners," Alexa pointed out. "The units were delivered here, and Tyler insisted that they be installed."

"Alexa, we both know Carrie well enough to know that she deals her own hand, so to speak. If she really wanted to blow off Tyler, she'd've single-handedly thrown those air conditioners out the windows and told him to get lost and stay lost. But she didn't!"

Ben flung himself down into a chair, draping his leg over the arm of it. "This Tyler Tremaine connection of Carrie's benefits both of us, too, you know."

Alexa rolled her eyes heavenward. "While I can see how being related to a Tremaine would be useful to you in your advertising career, it really has nothing to do with me."

"Yes, it does, Alexa. I've done some research on the Tremaines. Tyler just happens to have a younger brother who's single. Nathaniel Tremaine is thirty-two years old, handsome, bright and has never been married. Tyler and Carrie can arrange an introduction to him for you, and you can make your move. You're a knockout, sis. He'll fall for you like Tyler fell for Carrie, and then—"

"You're a lunatic, Ben," Alexa said, sighing with exasperation.

"I'm an optimist," Ben countered. "And maybe a bit of an opportunist, too, but that's not such a bad thing in these recessionary times." He glanced at his watch. "Well, if I'm not needed around here, I guess I'll be on my way. I have a date tonight."

"With Rhandee?"

"With Rhandee's roommate Darcy Lynn. I'm being passed around," he added rather proudly. He sauntered out, looking inordinately pleased with himself and the world in general.

"That's nothing to brag about, Ben," Alexa called after him, the disapproval in her tone unmistakable. Shaking her head, she reached for her book.

Nine

Ben's prediction that Tyler would be spending a lot of time in Carrie's newly air-conditioned house proved to be right on target. For the next several weeks, hardly a day went by that Carrie and the triplets didn't see Tyler. He arrived at their house after work to have dinner and spend the evening with them. They swam in his pool and he returned to their place for the children's bedtime rituals.

Tyler had always enjoyed business traveling, scheduling more trips than necessary, but now being away had lost its allure. He cut way back on his travel schedule, taking advantage of teleconferences and fax machines; it was more cost-efficient and, most importantly, it kept him in town. With Carrie.

He was in town on weekends, too, going to Carrie's house before she left for the hospital, and he invariably ended up staying with the children after she'd gone. Tyler struck up a genuine friendship with Alexa, but Ben, who sometimes dropped by, treated him with an ingratiating adulation that both irritated and amused him.

There was certainly nothing ingratiating or adulatory in the way Carrie treated him. If Tyler said or did something that she didn't like, she let him know it. Immediately. Still, considering their circumstances were so different, they were remarkably compatible and seemed to grow more so with each passing day. For two people who'd come from two such different worlds, they had a lot to talk about. Conversation flowed easily and naturally between them, but they also could be quietly companionable, enjoying each other in relaxed silence.

Not that silence reigned very often—not in a house with toddler triplets. The children were ever present, and Tyler's relationship with each one grew as the days flowed into weeks. He found himself looking forward to their greeting him at the door each evening, jabbering excitedly at the sight of him, pulling and tugging at him, demanding to be picked up. It was incredibly appealing to be welcomed so wholeheartedly, and Tyler found the entire "homecoming scene" impossible to resist.

He looked forward to seeing Carrie just as much, though she didn't fling herself at him at the door, the way her children did. But the sight of her smile and her blue eyes shining with warmth was a reward all its own. He'd thought she was attractive from the start, but she seemed to grow prettier daily. He found himself thinking about her often during the day, remembering previous conversations, anticipating new ones. In his head, he heard her laughter and saw the animation in her face, the alert intelligence gleaming in her eyes.

It was as if his mind had recorded and stored a thousand images of Carrie and he could call up any one of them as quickly as a computer locating a file. He visualized her face alive with tenderness and humor as she dealt with the triplets' antics, the way she rolled her eyes when Ben spouted one of his more outrageous lines. He saw her pensive and earnest and even flushed with anger. All the images interested and excited him, but when he pictured her dreamy-eyed, her lips moist and parted, her blue eyes intense with desire, the way she'd looked every time they had kissed, his blood heated and his body grew hard.

But though he wanted her more than he had ever wanted any woman during his prolonged bachelorhood, he had yet to take Carrie to bed. It was most un-Tremainelike behavior to deny himself what he wanted most, and Tyler was loath to question why his sex life had unexpectedly gone chaste.

He told himself that his constitution was unable to handle any more of the frustrating stop-starts that had plagued his and Carrie's earlier lovemaking attempts. If the children or Alexa or Ben weren't around to interrupt them, there was always the ghost of the sainted Ian Wilcox to be invoked, so why begin at all?

After all, there were viable alternatives to keeping his sexual energy in check. Tyler stepped up his exercise regime at his club, increased his racquetball, golf and tennis playing times and took frequent, lengthy cold showers. The other alternative, to cool his passion with other women while keeping his relationship with Carrie platonic, held no appeal for him. It was unthinkable—repugnant, even.

He was not only taking a sabbatical from dating, he also was taking a sabbatical from sex, Tyler decided. Now if only his celibate life-style would free him from his desire for the one woman he dreamed about day and night.

So far, it hadn't. The more time he spent with Carrie, the more he wanted her. She was affectionate by nature and seemed to think nothing of touching him, leaning against him, even throwing her arms around him for an occasional, spontaneous hug. Tyler responded in kind, draping his arm around her, taking her hand to hold. Not a day passed that didn't include some physical contact with Carrie, but Tyler didn't attempt to carry it further. He didn't pull her into his arms for one of those scorching kisses that had the power to send them both reeling. He might stare at the slender curve of her neck, at her breasts and her hips and her legs, but he didn't touch.

He didn't dare. The feelings he had for Carrie were so intense he sometimes felt overwhelmed, the emotions she evoked within him were so utterly unlike anything he had ever experienced that he didn't dare risk combining them with the ferocious power of sex. He'd never been as close to any woman as he was to Carrie, and adding passion and sex augured an intimacy he could not yet handle. Instead, he took refuge in the more comfortable fiction of his sexual sabbatical with his good friend and neighbor Carrie Shaw Wilcox.

The Fourth of July fell on a Wednesday, providing a holiday in the middle of the week, rather than the three-day holiday weekend Tyler would have preferred. Still, he had plans which he shared with Carrie.

"I have a beach house in Rehoboth. Just a small place, nothing fancy," he told her the Monday evening before the holiday, as they floated side by side in his pool. She was pulling Emily on a pink plastic surfboard with a built-in seat, and he tugged Franklin and Dylan in the little blow-up boat. "Since you finally have a weekend off, I thought we'd take the kids down there. We can leave Friday night and come back Sunday evening."

He didn't add that he hadn't been to the beach at all this summer, that he'd been fielding calls from friends, acquaintances and would-be sycophants who wanted to know why Tyler Tremaine, usually a weekend fixture at the Delaware shore and a major player on the summer party scene, had been conspicuously absent from his seasonal stomping grounds. If they all knew he'd been spending his weekends with his next-door neighbor's children—while their mother was at work—they wouldn't have believed it. Sometimes, *he* still didn't believe it, either.

"We'll leave late Friday, to beat the weekend traffic on the Bay Bridge," Tyler continued. "Around ten o'clock."

Carrie pushed her wet hair from her face. "Oh, Tyler, I don't think so."

"They'll love it, Carrie. The house is right on the beach. They can play in the sand and in the ocean and there's a small boardwalk with kiddie rides and—"

"But it takes over two hours to get there. They've never been in a car for that long a drive. And where will they sleep and eat, once we're there? There are no cribs or high chairs. It would be impossible. No, Tyler. Thank you, but we just can't—"

"Carrie, we're going," he said firmly. "I've been thinking about it. These children never go anywhere, not even to the supermarket. And while I can understand how it would've been overwhelming—and way too difficult—to take them out when they were infants, they're getting older now."

"They come here, to your pool," Carrie reminded him. "You even let them inside your house now and then," she added, smiling.

"And think how much they love to come over here, because it's a change, it's something different. They're bright, curious kids and they should be exposed to other things, to other places and more people. They'll be stunted, emotionally and intellectually, if they never leave their house and don't see anyone but you and me and Alexa and Ben."

She stared at him thoughtfully. "I—think you might be right. No, I know you are. In fact, what you've said sounds like something my father might say."

"You mean I'm on the same wavelength as Colonel Shaw?" Tyler feigned shock. "Now there's food for thought."

Carrie laughed. "Don't let Ben's exaggerated stories about Dad fool you. My father is very smart and very strong. You'd like him. In fact, I think the two of you are a lot alike."

"High praise indeed from a dyed-in-the-wool daddy's girl," Tyler said lightly. "Alexa and Ben have told me more than once that you're the colonel's favorite."

Carrie splashed water at him. "That's absurd. Our parents have no favorites. What other stuff do you and Alexa and Ben talk about when I'm not around to defend myself?"

"Mmm, wouldn't you like to know?" he teased. "So, we're on for this weekend then? We can rent cribs and high chairs down there. As for the length of the drive... since we'll be leaving later, the kids will probably sleep the whole way."

Carrie nodded her head. "Tyler, do you think I'm overprotective?" she asked a moment later. "You know, a—a smothering type of mother?"

"Of course not. It's natural for the mother to want to keep her babies close."

"And I guess it's the father's role to make sure the kids get to interact with others and get out of the nest and into the world little by little," Carrie replied, then realized what she'd said, how it sounded. *Tyler was not her children's father!*

It would be a grave mistake on her part to let herself think of him as a surrogate daddy. After all, he had told her in no uncertain terms that he didn't want to play that role. But that seemed like ages ago; words spoken by another man about hypothetical children that had nothing to do with Tyler and the triplets.

These past weeks, she and the children had come to count on Tyler being around, to look forward to seeing him stride up the walk or through the gap in the backyard hedge at the end of his workday. On the rare evenings he had late meetings or business-related dinners, they missed him. Terribly.

Carrie didn't ask Tyler why he was spending so much time with them. She suspected that he himself didn't know, that being with her and the triplets was something of a lark or a whim for him. A temporary one, to be sure, despite Ben's embarrassingly obvious expectations for the relationship. Carrie entertained no such delusions; though she knew she was in love with Tyler, she foresaw no fairy-tale ending.

Only an ending. A painful one for both her and the triplets who loved "Ty," too. What were they going to do when he stopped coming? And he'd stop coming sooner rather than later, if she continued to blurt out heavy-duty "daddy" expectations such as that last comment!

Carrie glanced furtively at Tyler. He was fetching a toy for Dylan, chatting with both boys. Apparently he'd taken her remark as hypothetical and not pertaining personally to himself. Thank heavens for that!

But Carrie was wrong. Her words were echoing in Tyler's head. *A father's role? Is that what he'd been playing with the Wilcox triplets?*

Franklin chose that moment to stand up in the boat, and it toppled over, spilling both boys into the water. They bounced upright, laughing, buoyed by their life jackets, and Tyler caught them and plunked them back in the boat before Carrie could reach them. *Very smart and very strong... a father's role...*

And then: "Oh, he—drat!" Tyler exclaimed and was thankful he'd caught himself because Emily, that little parrot, yelled "Drat!" at the top of her lungs. Her siblings immediately picked up the chant.

"All this talk about fathers made me think of my own," Tyler said grimacing. "He and his wife want me to come out to his place on the Fourth, this Wednesday evening. How would you and the kids like to go along, Carrie? Sort of a test run for the beach excursion, although I promise we'll have a much better time at the beach than with the Tremaines."

He was inviting her to meet his family? But that milestone paled in light of their intimidating identity. They were the *Tremaines!* "We'd love to come," Carrie said quickly, before she could chicken out and refuse.

"An invitation from Richard Tremaine is really a combined executive, paternal command," Tyler explained as he drove Carrie and the triplets to the Tremaine estate in an exclusive Maryland suburb. "I'm glad you and the kids are joining me for Dad and Nina's foolhardy attempt at a good old-fashioned holiday picnic."

Carrie stole a quick glance at him. She was still surprised he had invited her and the children to meet his family—although knowing Tyler, he hadn't viewed it in that context. He'd said they were his hedge against boredom and an excuse to make an early exit from the monstrously dull and stilted Tremaine faux family event.

"Why *faux* family?" Carrie asked, and for the first time since they'd discussed his mother's death in her kitchen all those weeks ago, Tyler talked about the Tremaine family, not Tremaine Incorporated.

"This one-big-happy-family pretense is phony and fake, no matter how much Dad and Nina might want it to be otherwise." Tyler scowled. "Nina is my father's second wife, he married her a couple years ago. She was a widow with a son and two daughters and Dad was the perennial widower. He'd dated over the years, of course, but according to legend he was too much in love with his dearly departed wife—my mother—to ever consider marrying again."

"Your mother died a long time ago, Tyler," Carrie pointed out quietly. She glanced back at the triplets, playing quietly with small toys as they sat strapped into their car safety seats, all in a line. They'd taken Carrie's car, which was equipped to transport children. Tyler's collectible cars did not meet that requirement.

Would her children expect her to dedicate her entire life to the memory of their father? She recalled that she'd actually planned to do just that . . . until Tyler Tremaine had made living in the present so much more compelling than living in the past. Carrie stared at his profile, her cheeks flushing. "Do you really think that your father—uh—betrayed her memory because he married another woman three decades later?"

"My father didn't betray my mother's memory, he betrayed her while she was still alive," Tyler said bitterly. "He had an affair with Nina when my brother Cole was just a baby."

"Oh." Carrie gulped. "That does sound sleazy."

"It gets worse," Tyler assured her. "Nina got pregnant, and according to Dad's current revisionist history, he wanted to divorce his wife and marry his mistress. Noble Nina, however, would have no part in home-wrecking—like she hadn't already done so by sleeping with a married man! Anyway, she got some poor sucker by the name of McKay to marry her and raise the kid as his own. Dad went back to his wife and had two more sons, Nathaniel and me, and Nina eventually had two daughters by McKay. When our mother was killed in that car crash, Dad hightailed it to Nina and begged her to dump her husband and marry him. When she didn't, he donned the role of the bereaved widower who refused to ever marry again. But it wasn't my poor mother he was mourning, it was the fact that he couldn't have Nina."

"And you grew up not knowing any of this?"

Tyler nodded. "Yeah, I completely bought Dad's tragic-loss-of-his-beloved-Marnie tale. The truth all came out when my—my *half brother* Connor McKay surfaced two years ago."

"You have a half brother you never even knew existed," Carrie exclaimed, awed. "Things like that happen all the time on daytime soap operas but—"

"You can imagine how pleased I was to find myself living a plot line right out of 'All My Children,'" Tyler said wryly. "As for Dad, he certainly has a lot of children these days. Four sons and two stepdaughters and their various offspring. Connor—who incidentally took a job with Tremaine Incorporated and legally took the name Tremaine as well—is married with a little girl and another baby on the way. Nina's two daughters are married with children, as well."

"Correct me if I'm wrong, but the fact that Connor is a Tremaine, and has claimed his birthright and his name, disturbs you more than your father's marriage to Nina," Carrie said shrewdly. "You view him as a potential rival in Tremaine Incorporated."

"I'd be an idiot if I didn't," Tyler said roughly. "I want to be president of the company and I've worked damn hard to achieve that goal. When Dad retires and Cole steps up as chairman, the presidency is supposed to be mine."

"And Connor wants to be president of the company, too?" Carrie asked. "Oh, dear, this is getting complicated."

"He says he doesn't," Tyler admitted. "Connor claims he'll be happy heading the legal department as Tremaine's General Counsel. He insists he has no further corporate ambitions."

"But you don't believe him?"

Tyler shrugged. "Connor's a bright guy. And his mother is finally married to his father who wants to do anything—everything!—to make up for all those missing years."

"That would hardly include handing Connor the presidency of the company when you've worked hard for it all these years," Carrie said reasonably. "What about your brothers Cole and Nathaniel? Do they feel threatened, too?"

"Cole's position is unassailable, he's the oldest son. As for Nathaniel..." Tyler laughed shortly. "Hey, I know my kid brother has a brain but he doesn't care to exercise it in the business world. He has a window-dressing job with the company and not an ounce of ambition to advance to a position with any authority or responsibility. He's the family goof-off who takes long vacations, skips meetings and does what he feels like doing when he feels like doing it."

"No competition there," Carrie agreed. "I guess Nathaniel lost to his older brothers enough as a kid to know he's not supposed to succeed, so why bother to try?"

Tyler clenched his jaw. "Carrie, please skip the instant armchair analysis. I know Tremaine Books sells volumes on the subject, but I happen to loathe psychobabble."

Carrie was undaunted. "I read a very interesting book on birth order, and one whole chapter was devoted to stepfamilies and the problems that arise when siblings feel that their place in the family has been usurped."

"Usurped?" Tyler echoed. He found himself grinning in spite of himself. Carrie's earnest intensity on topics he found ridiculous never failed to amuse him. "Help! My enviable position of middle son has been usurped! Call in the shrinks!"

He reached over and patted her knee lightly. "On the other hand, I'm glad you've switched from reading terrifying thrillers to pop psychology claptrap. They won't keep you awake at night—just the opposite, in fact. Instant sedation."

Carrie laid her hand on top of his, eyeing him from beneath her lashes, waiting for him to withdraw his hand, wishing fervently that he wouldn't.

And he didn't. Whether it was a friendly gesture of affection or a sexual overture, Carrie wasn't sure, but Tyler linked his thumb with hers and rested his big hand on her knee for the rest of the drive.

Carrie was stunned by her first sight of Richard Tremaine's estate, the place where Tyler and his brothers had been raised. "The house is the size of some neighborhoods I've lived in," she said uneasily. She'd never seen any house so enormous, so grand.

She smoothed the cherry-and-white-striped material of her wide-cut shorts with nervous fingers. She wore a rayon shirt that matched the shorts, and until she'd spied the palatial house, she'd considered herself well-turned-out for the picnic. Now she wasn't so sure. This place seemed to call for diamonds and silk and fur, even if it was July!

"Now, don't go getting awestruck by the Tremaine trappings," Tyler said mockingly. "I get enough fawning and groveling from your brother, Ben."

Carrie's cheeks pinked. Ben did tend to fawn and grovel; he made no secret of his admiration for anything Tremaine. And if Ben were to see this place, he would probably drop to his knees and salaam. Nervously, she turned her attention to freeing the triplets from their car seats as Tyler parked in the long, wide, circular drive. A small private roadway led to the house, which could not even be seen from the main road.

The triplets were wearing matching outfits, red-and-white-striped shorts and bright blue shirts printed with white stars, holiday presents from their doting grandparents overseas. Emily had a red barrette clipped in her ever-tousled blond hair, a touch of femininity to distinguish her from her brothers. All three children insisted on walking rather than being carried, so Tyler and Carrie took their hands and they walked five abreast to the pillared entrance of the mansion.

When the massive front door was opened by a uniformed butler, Carrie had to suppress a nervous giggle. The man even had the requisite British accent; he looked like

Central Casting's stereotypical upper-class servant. But her laughter and the remark she was about to make to Tyler died on her lips when a beautiful fifty-something blonde, dressed in an exquisite gown and clinging to the arm of a tall, silver-haired gentleman wearing a tuxedo, appeared in the spacious tile-and-marble vestibule.

"Hello, Dad. Hello, Nina," Tyler said, cordial but cool. "Meet the Wilcoxes—Carrie, Dylan, Emily and Franklin."

He didn't specify who was whom, but Carrie was too appalled by her own incredibly inappropriate outfit to notice. By now, several other men and women, doubtless the younger Tremaines and their spouses, had joined them, and their attire matched that of Nina and Richard Tremaine. All the women wore what Carrie knew must be fabulously expensive dresses and impressive jewelry; all the men wore tuxes.

She cast a horrified glance at Tyler, who was wearing cutoff jeans and a navy-and-white T-shirt, sans logo, far removed from even a designer polo shirt. He didn't even look preppy; he looked as out of place among these richly attired folk as she did!

"Mommy!" Emily whimpered, clutching her mother's leg, obviously unnerved by the crowd of strangers gathering. Carrie put her arm around her daughter. The smallest Tremaines were nowhere to be seen. Tyler had said there would be a slew of youngsters about, but Carrie knew beyond a doubt that there would be no children at this affair. It was a formal party, for adults only...and she had arrived with her toddlers, dressed for a backyard cookout.

She cast Tyler a half pleading, half accusatory look. How could he have done this to her! But Tyler didn't appear to have a single qualm. He smilingly draped his arm around her shoulder and began to introduce her to a sea of faces, all of which blurred before her mortified eyes.

Cole, Chelsea, Connor, Courtney, Cristine—as if the sheer number of elegantly attired people wasn't intimidat-

ing and confusing enough, they all had names that began
with the letter *C!* Was this some sort of joke? Carrie was
relieved to meet non-*C*'s Monica, Jeff, Tom and Nathaniel, but she was too rattled to put together all the names and
faces.

Everybody had polite smiles pasted on their faces, but
Carrie couldn't summon a smile in response, not even a false
one. Her expression mirrored her children's—wary and
watchful and very uncertain.

"Tyler, you haven't met Nina's nieces from Chicago,"
Richard Tremaine said in those cool but commanding tones
of his. Two tall, brown-eyed blondes in short, strapless, sequined dresses stepped forward to be presented. The elder
Tremaine introduced them as Brooke and Rae Ann Raleigh.

Carrie watched the two women fawn over "Uncle Richard," then move on to Tyler. "I guess we're cousins now,"
one of them said, tittering. "Kissin' cousins," said the other.
They'd achieved the impossible, Carrie noted wryly; the
gushing Raleigh sisters actually made Ben look subtle!

"It was absolutely wonderful of Aunt Nina and Uncle
Richard to have this dinner dance to welcome us to Maryland," Rae Ann Raleigh breathed, her eyes predatorily
feasting on Tyler.

"You and your sister are most delightful guests of honor,
my dear," Richard said gallantly.

"All the other guests are out on the terrace," Nathaniel
Tremaine put in, his eyes gleaming wickedly. "Everybody's
been asking about you, Tyler."

Dinner dance! With additional guests on the terrace? It
was as if she'd stumbled into an F. Scott Fitzgerald novel—
dressed all wrong. Carrie stared at Tyler, her eyes glimmering with homicidal intent. Tyler had claimed this was a casual family picnic, not a formal dinner dance. And the
"delightful" guests of honor were obviously to be partnered by Nina's eligible stepsons, Tyler and Nathaniel.

Was that why Tyler had brought her and the triplets along? To circumvent Nina's plans and ruin her party? Tyler had made his feelings about his father's wife quite clear. It didn't take a great leap of the imagination to figure that he might deliberately try to sabotage Nina's party. Carrie felt sick. The fact that he would use her and her children to do it was a crushing blow.

They had to leave, Carrie decided. Immediately. She would make her apologies to Richard and Nina Tremaine, take the kids and get out of here. But before she could say a word, a boisterous black Labrador retriever came bounding down the grand staircase and hurled itself into the middle of the group.

"Marquis has escaped!" Nina Tremaine laughed with nervous gaiety and tried to grab the dog by its collar. "He's just a puppy and so full of energy."

Marquis may have been just a puppy but he was quite a bit larger than the triplets who had instantly and joyously attracted his canine attention. Marquis jumped eagerly at Dylan, knocking him off his feet, then began to lick the little boy's face while he lay on the ground. There was a buzz of concerned voices, but Carrie, acting immediately, caught the dog by the collar and pulled him away.

Dylan sat up, laughing. "Big dog!" he said admiringly.

Emily did not share her brother's aplomb. Though constrained by Carrie, Marquis was leaping and yipping, and the little girl let out a piercing scream and burst into hysterical tears. "Big dog!" she shrieked, her interpretation of the phrase very different from Dylan's. In a frenzy of fear, she held up her arms to Tyler to be rescued from the menacing beast.

Tyler scooped up the baby in his arms. "Will someone get that damned dog out of here!" he thundered. "He's terrified Emily."

An apologetic Nina took the dog from Carrie and led him off. Carrie picked up Dylan and tried to wipe the doggy kisses from his small cheeks. It was at that moment that she noticed Franklin was no longer standing at her left side.

"Franklin?" Carrie called. "I—I don't see him," she explained, feeling panic sweep through her.

No one saw Franklin. He wasn't in the vestibule.

"Connor, go check the swimming pool!" exclaimed his very pregnant wife, Courtney, her eyes wide with concern. Connor took off in a run. A few others scattered as well.

"He couldn't have made it to the pool," Tyler assured Carrie. "It's too far for him to walk from here. Anyway, the pool area is completely fenced in."

Pandemonium was close, but had not quite set in when Nathaniel reappeared to announce, "There's a kid dressed like the American flag sitting in the middle of the dining room table."

Everybody headed to the dining room, Carrie among the last, because she had no idea where the dining room was and had to follow the crowd. Judging by the length of time it took to reach the room, she feared it might be in another county.

She heard murmurs of disapproval mixed with those of amusement before she actually saw the scene, that had captured everyone's attention. There was Franklin sitting in the middle of the immense table, munching on something, his path clearly traceable from the overturned chair to the china and silver askew.

Before anyone could reach him, the little boy stretched out one leg, accidentally kicking the large crystal vase, which was filled with an artful arrangement of fresh flowers. Carrie watched it all happen as if in slow motion. The vase tipped over, spilling water and flowers over the impeccably set table.

"Uh-oh!" Franklin crowed. He took in stride the fact that he was now sitting in a puddle, splashing the water with his small hands. "Wet," he observed importantly. It was a new word and he said it again, louder. "Wet!"

Carrie groaned. Someone retrieved her son and put him in her arms. Dylan, whom she was also holding, reached over to touch his brother. "Wet," he affirmed.

Connor Tremaine, out of breath from his run, arrived to announce, "The baby's not anywhere near the pool."

"No, he's here. He decided to swim in the dining room instead," Cole Tremaine said dryly.

Everybody laughed. Emily, still wailing in Tyler's arms, pumped up her volume, effectively drowning out the laughter with her cries. Carrie felt every eye upon them. Someday, she would laugh about this herself, she silently promised, but right now that day seemed light years away.

"We're going home," she announced.

The crowd parted to let her through. Certainly no one was going to stop her or insist that she stay. She raced back toward the entrance, carrying Franklin and Dylan in her arms. The young brothers seemed to be discussing their evening out. Through the buzzing in her ears, Carrie heard them repeating "dog" and "wet" several times.

"Incredible! I can't believe that Tyler actually did it!" Nathaniel Tremaine materialized at her elbow, keeping pace with her as she rushed to the door. "Who are you, really? Did Tyler hire you and those kids from the same agency that shoots commercials for us?"

"What are you talking about?" Carrie muttered, not breaking her stride.

"You don't have to pretend with me," Nathaniel jovially assured her. "I know my brother hired you to show up here tonight as his date—and adding all those kids was a master touch! Wow! Tyler warned Dad that he'd had it with their meddling matchmaking, and trying to fix him up with Nina's heinous nieces was the last straw! He definitely made his point tonight. I bet Dad will stop hounding him now! So what's the going rate for a gig like this?"

"Ten thousand dollars," Carrie said tightly. "I keep half and the rest is split among the kids. We've worked together before. The agency saw the resemblance between all of us and took full advantage of it. Just look at the three children, wouldn't you swear they were blood relatives?''

Nathaniel peered closely at Dylan and Franklin. "I sure would. These two look like twins."

"The miracles of proper casting," Carrie said succinctly. They reached the vestibule and the butler politely swung open the door for her. "Would you do me a favor?" she asked Nathaniel. "Get the other baby from your brother and take her to my car for me? Our work here is through."

"I'll do you a favor, if you'll do one for me," Nathaniel said smoothly. "I want your phone number. I don't want to hire you—I'd like to go out with you."

Carrie looked at him archly. "Why not ask one of Nina's nieces out instead? I'm sure your new kissin' cousins will be only too happy to go anywhere with you."

She strode to her car. If only she and the children could be magically teleported out of here, she thought grimly as she buckled Dylan and Franklin into their car seats. She didn't want to even look at Tyler, but since he had Emily, she was forced to acknowledge his presence.

He was behind her now, and she snatched her still-sniffling daughter from him, her blue eyes flashing fire. "You can go back to the party now," she snapped. "I'm sure nobody will mind that you're a tad underdressed for it." Least of all those two slavering nieces with dollar signs in their eyes.

Tyler had the nerve to laugh. "Some Fourth of July picnic, huh?"

"How could you, Tyler?" Carrie turned on him, having safely strapped all three children inside the car. "I understand you resenting your father's and Nina's matchmaking attempts, but to—to use us this way, to make fools of us!" She was horrified that her eyes had filled with tears and she stubbornly blinked them away.

Tyler stared at her. It was finally dawning on him that she failed to see the humor in the situation. "I didn't use you," he protested. "Carrie, you don't think that I deliberately misled you about tonight, do you? Because I didn't."

Carrie slipped behind the steering wheel, keeping her eyes focused straight ahead. She couldn't bear to look at the traitor. "You didn't know this was a formal dinner dance? You thought it was a casual family picnic, complete with kids running around in the backyard and hot dogs on the grill?"

"Yeah," Tyler replied rather belligerently. "I did. That's a fairly typical way to spend the Fourth of July, isn't it? We'd done it that way last year, but I guess Nina's pretentious social ambitions have advanced since then, not to mention her two gold-digging nieces hoping to jump aboard the Tremaine gravy train themselves."

"You actually expect me to believe that you weren't told what kind of an affair this was? Especially since you and your brother are the door prizes for *Aunt Nina's* and *Uncle Richard's* guests of honor?" She turned the key in the ignition. "Don't insult my intelligence, Tyler."

"I wouldn't dream of it. Slide over, I'll drive," Tyler decreed, and tried to shove her toward the passenger side, so he could get behind the wheel.

Carrie didn't budge. "I'm driving," she said so fiercely that even Tyler recognized the wisdom in not pushing her.

"Okay," he said carefully. "You drive. I'll ride shotgun." He started to walk around the car.

Carrie gunned the engine. The moment after he'd passed in front of the car, she took off, tires peeling, sending gravel flying. She caught a glimpse of a stunned Tyler in the rearview mirror, watching their getaway.

From the back seat came a mournful wail. "Ty!" It was Emily, and when there was no response, she burst into tears, her cries a mixture of sadness and rage.

Carrie knew how she felt, but there was little she could do to console her child while driving the car. "Let's listen to some songs," she said with ghastly false cheer, switching on the radio in an attempt to divert all of them.

It was either an unfortunate coincidence or pure fate that "Achy, Breaky Heart" blared through the speakers. Carrie's own heart felt heavy as lead in her chest. It was over with Tyler; it had to be over.

Tonight he'd shown what he really thought of them: that they were convenient pawns to be used in his power struggle with his father, that their very presence ensured a ruined evening. The triplets were too young to realize the unattractive role they'd been cast in, and if Carrie should feel hurt and humiliated and betrayed . . .

Well, what concern was that to a heartbreaker like Tyler Tremaine?

Ten

They had crossed the District line when Carrie realized that she was being followed. A sleek black car—she was uncertain of the make, but it looked sporty and masculine and very expensive—was directly behind her and stayed there, changing lanes when she did, exiting the beltway after her, making the same turns onto the city streets. She knew who was riding in that supercharged machine though not who was behind the wheel of it. None other than Tyler himself.

Apparently, he was seeking the very confrontation she'd been hoping to avoid. Her nerves were taut, her stomach churning, by the time she pulled up in front of her house. Moments later, the black car pulled alongside her.

Tyler sprang from the passenger side. "Thanks, Connor," he called, slamming the car door. Connor zoomed away with a jaunty honk of the horn.

"Connor drove you?" Carrie blurted out. She was immediately annoyed with herself. She'd fully intended to freeze out Tyler with icy silence. Well, so much for that plan; she might as well move on to sarcasm now. "You actually deigned to accept a ride from your allegedly scheming half brother?"

Tyler nodded sheepishly. "I guess that must tell you something about how much I—"

"It tells me that you're willing to use anyone to serve your purposes," Carrie cut in. "Both enemies and friends."

"You managed to miss the point entirely," Tyler said cryptically. "But maybe it's for the best."

They worked together in tense silence, lifting the triplets out of the car and shepherding them into the house. Emily clung to Tyler like a baby monkey, and when Carrie tried to take her from him, the little traitor howled her protest.

"Don't worry, honey, Ty will stay right here with you," Tyler said, ostensibly to Emily, though he was looking smugly at Carrie as he spoke.

"It's past their bedtime but they have to have dinner first since they didn't get anything to eat at that bogus picnic of yours," Carrie said coldly.

"Franklin did," Tyler drawled. "I saw him chomping on some of Nina's flower arrangement."

Carrie glared at him. "You think this is all a great big joke, don't you? It doesn't matter to you that I was mortified to show up there, uninvited and—"

"*I* invited you!"

"But you neglected to mention that fact to either Nina or your father. All part of your nasty little plan, I suppose. Spring the kids and me on your unsuspecting relatives for full shock value."

"You're reading way too much into this, Carrie. I didn't—"

"Tyler, just shut up!" Her voice was too low for the triplets to hear and gleefully parrot, but the fierce intensity of her words was not masked.

With the toddlers in their high chairs, gnawing on bread, Carrie put together a meal for them. Tyler watched her intently. Her back was ramrod straight; she was tense as a tightly wound spring. She didn't say a word to him, didn't glance his way until after she'd served the children their dinner.

Finally, she turned to face him. Her blue eyes were glacial. "Are you still here?" she asked, her tone as arctic as her stare.

"I'm not going anywhere, Carrie." He folded his arms and lounged against the counter, his pose deceptively casual. His feelings were anything but casual; he felt wired and wild.

"The game is over, Tyler," she said flatly.

"Do you mind telling me exactly what game it is we're playing? Tag? You ran and I caught you. Hide-and-seek? You came back here to your place to hide and I found you."

"I think it's charades," snapped Carrie. "I'm supposed to guess what part you're playing now. Well, forget it. I can't. You're too accomplished an actor."

"And what's that supposed to mean?"

"It means that I—I quit. Our friendship—if that's what it is or ever was—is over. I'm not going to let you use me and my children as ammunition in your adolescent feud with your father and his wife. From now on, you're no longer welcome to come over here and kill time with us while you're waiting for your—your self-imposed exile from the social scene to end."

"You don't want to see me anymore?" Tyler stared at her in disbelief. There was a roaring in his ears, and his every muscle was tensed. "Is that what you're trying to say, Carrie?"

"I'm not trying, I'm saying it!"

"All because of a stupid picnic that—"

"There was no picnic!" cried Carrie. "And you knew it!"

"Carrie, listen to me." Tyler gritted through clenched teeth. "Nina invited me to the house on the Fourth, saying that my father especially wanted me to come, thereby making it mandatory, not optional, that I show up. After she said that, I stopped listening to her. I completely tuned her out. I assumed it would be the same lousy picnic as last year. Maybe she told me it was a formal dinner dance—she probably did—but I wasn't paying any attention. I make it a point not to listen to Nina while she yaks on and on.''

''I suppose you didn't know that her nieces were to be there either,'' Carrie said scornfully.

Tyler grimaced. ''I did know about them because Nathaniel called me to complain. Neither of us wanted to meet them. We figured that being Nina's nieces, they probably had all the charm of Cinderella's stepsisters. I decided to bring you and the kids with me because I wanted all of them, the entire family, to know that—''

''—you were sick and tired of being the object of their meddling,'' Carrie finished for him. ''And that their punishment for this particular matchmaking attempt was to bring in the junior wrecking crew to demolish the party.''

She thought of Franklin on the well-appointed table, the lovely centerpiece ruined along with Lord knows what else and of Emily's nonstop screaming. The junior wrecking crew had certainly given it their best shot. But she couldn't blame the babies. It was all Tyler's fault. She glowered balefully at him.

Tyler's lips thinned into a straight line. What he'd been about to blurt out had shocked him as much as it would've astonished Carrie, had she let him say it. He'd almost told her that he had wanted his family to meet the woman and children with whom he'd been spending all his spare time, that he wanted them all to know he was not available for matchmaking, no matter what or with whom.

He was no longer eligible. He was seriously involved with Carrie Shaw Wilcox, mother of three. He was in love with a woman he hadn't even taken to bed yet! And if that wasn't enough, she was looking at him as if she hated him. She'd already told him she didn't want to see him again.

He pulled out a chair and sat down hard. "Well, this is a helluva mess."

"You're finally willing to concede that what you did was cruel and rude and completely unfeeling?" Carrie demanded.

"I'm willing to concede that I screwed up by mistaking the damn dinner dance for a picnic. But I still don't think it's the capital offense you're making it out to be, Carrie. I mean, look at me. I'm not exactly dressed for a formal party, either, but I didn't feel humiliated because everybody else was running around in tuxes."

"You were undoubtedly proud of yourself," Carrie agreed acidly. "It fits the in-your-face statement you were trying to make."

Tyler sighed exasperatedly. "Damn, you're stubborn! Why won't you let yourself believe me? I didn't take you to my father's house to shock him or to humiliate you. I didn't get the attire straight and you were embarrassed in front of the others, and for that I sincerely apologize. But I think you owe me an apology too, Carrie."

"Me? For what?"

"For all your name-calling and accusations, which are both untrue and unfounded."

"That's not the way I see it." A chaotic blend of anger and pain swirled inside her. "I think it's best that you leave now, Tyler."

He stood up. "So you think that's best, do you? I wonder how the kids will feel about it?"

"If you try to drag them into this, you'll simply prove my point that you're willing to use them to advance your own agenda."

"My own agenda," Tyler repeated wryly, rising to his feet. "Right. I'll do anything to promote it, won't I?" Too bad he didn't even know what it was.

Carrie talked as if he'd actually planned all of this, step-by-step, from his deepening involvement with her and her family to tonight's debacle with his family. Wouldn't she be surprised to know that he was completely off balance and floundering for the first time in his life? In love for the first time in his life. And while she seemed to have all the answers, he was clueless. Anger surged through him. At least she didn't know *that,* and he was not about to tell her. His pride demanded that he pretend to be the Machiavellian sharpie that she considered him to be.

He left quietly, deliberately not attracting the triplets' attention so as not to have to stave off their objections. And he knew they would have protested his departure, had they noticed. Those kids loved him, even if their exasperating, pugnacious, thoroughly maddening mother had decided he was the worst kind of calculating fiend.

Maybe he should post watch outside his garage, in case brother Ben came skulking by with his trusty box of sugar. That was the way the intrepid Shaw triplets dealt with those who offended them, wasn't it? And they probably saw no reason to differentiate between real and imagined slights, either. Seething with self-righteous indignation, Tyler stormed into his house.

He savored the peace and quiet for a full ten minutes before the absolute silence struck him as unnerving. He put some favorite music in his CD player to break the oppressive quietude, but the lack of voices and laughter and even squalling made the place seem lifeless and empty.

He gazed down at the house next door, which was blazing with lights. He was not depressed, Tyler assured himself. He was simply readjusting. In no time at all, he'd be enjoying himself and relishing his return to the fun-filled, peripatetic way of life he had so foolishly abandoned all those weeks ago.

When the phone rang two hours later, Carrie raced to answer it. "Oh, hi, Alexa." Though she tried, she couldn't keep the disappointment from her voice. She'd been hoping, praying, that Tyler would call.

"I wanted to find out how tonight went, meeting the Tremaines and all, but I guess I called at a bad time." Alexa sounded apologetic.

"Not at all. Tonight was awful, just awful. And worst of all, I—I think I blew everything out of proportion and overreacted." Carrie gulped back the lump that seemed to have lodged permanently in her throat since Tyler's departure. "Oh, Alexa, I know I did. After Tyler left, I started thinking about what happened and what he'd said and—"

"Tyler left?"

"I threw him out," Carrie confessed glumly. "I told him I didn't want to see him anymore and he—he went, Alexa!"

"Oh, Carrie!"

"Please, no lectures. I'll be getting enough of that from Ben," Carrie said with a woeful stab at gallows humor.

"I'm not going to lecture you, Carrie. Do you want me to come over?"

"No, I—I'll be okay." It wasn't fair for her to expect her sister to always come running to her side; Alexa deserved a break from her self-imposed misery. "I really will," she said, hoping to sound more convincing.

"I think I'm going to read awhile before I go to bed. Don't worry about me, Alexa. Promise that you won't."

The moment they hung up, Alexa called Ben. "I just want to warn you not to go into your usual raves about Tyler if you happen to call Carrie," Alexa told her brother. "They're having problems."

"What? Oh, no, this is terrible!" Ben howled. "What happened?"

"I don't know anything except Carrie is sorry about it. I don't think she's sure enough of him to call him and apologize, either."

"They love each other, *I'm* sure of that. Sounds like they could use a little help admitting and committing, though."

"Stop talking in ad jingles," Alexa scolded. "And don't give Carrie a hard time about Tyler."

"I wouldn't dream of it," Ben said earnestly. "I want Carrie to be happy as much as you do, Alexa."

"I know, Ben."

Carrie put on her blue silk nightshirt, styled like an oversize man's shirt, and stretched out on the sofa with a magazine. The doorbell rang ten minutes later.

Her limbs shaking, her heart thudding, Carrie walked to the door and peered through the peephole. Tyler stood outside.

"I decided to give you another chance," he said the moment she opened the door.

He was pleased with his delivery. He sounded cool and insouciant, nothing at all like the lovesick jerk who'd spent the past two hours manically pacing his house, trying and failing to imagine his days without Carrie in them. It was time she shared his nights, too. Still, a lifetime of fierce male pride made swallowing it difficult. He waited, tense and edgy. Now that he'd made the overture, if she were to spurn him again...

"That's funny. I was going to call you and tell you the same thing," Carrie said, her voice as shaky as her knees. The moisture gathering in her eyes made them shine like brilliant jewels.

"You were, hmm?" Tyler stepped inside and closed the door firmly behind him, locking it.

Carrie looked at the ground. "I—It's possible that you thought it really was a picnic," she murmured.

"You're willing to entertain the possibility that you weren't the victim of a diabolical scheme I purposely hatched to infuriate the Tremaines en masse?"

Carrie raised her eyes to meet his. He was watching her with his usual intensity but she detected something else there, as well. "Yes," she whispered. A slow, sweet smile turned up the corners of her mouth. "Although you would've been justified in hatching any plot to save yourself from those—those bleached blond wolverines Nina calls her nieces."

For a moment, Tyler looked at her as if he didn't believe his ears. Then he smiled. "Wolverines?" he repeated, laughing. His dark green eyes gleamed with an unmistakable, irresistible combination of humor and passion.

Carrie shuddered as she was overtaken by simultaneous waves of tears and laughter. Her guard, so zealously maintained, dropped; her staunch control was swept away in a maelstrom of emotion. She flung her arms around Tyler's neck. "I love you, Tyler," she said, stretching on tiptoe to kiss him. "I just want you to know—"

"I know," he said huskily. "I know, sweetheart."

His arms closed around her and his lips claimed hers in a deep, searing kiss. Colors seemed to explode inside Carrie's head like a dazzling rainbow as she tasted him, welcoming his tongue into her mouth with erotic strokes of her own, making love to his mouth as hungrily as he was making love to hers. It had been so long since he had kissed her, and all the fierce, suppressed yearning for him swelled within her and burst forth with head-spinning pleasure.

Tyler was reeling from a similar surge of pent-up longings. He had wanted her for weeks, and finally his desires and his needs were totally unleashed and coursing madly through his body. His hunger for Carrie was wild and raging and all-consuming.

His mouth was hot and hard and urgently demanding, and Carrie's heart lunged excitedly as she realized that he was as out of control as she. Their kiss grew wilder, deeper, and very, very soon kissing, however intimate, was not enough for either of them.

With a rough sound of passion, Tyler slid his hands under her nightshirt, raising the hem and gliding his palms over her thighs, her panties, sliding upward to close over her breasts. He kneaded the rounded softness, rubbing his fingertips over her nipples until they were so taut and so sensitive that she wanted to scream with the exquisite, piercing pleasure of it.

Desire escalated and swept through her like wildfire, heightening her responses, making her breathing ragged and her body soft and pliant. Locked against the long, hard length of his body, she could feel the powerful thrust of his male arousal, and she arched even more closely into him, instinctively rocking against him in seductive, feminine rhythm.

His mouth left hers for only a moment before he urgently reclaimed it. They were both panting, but neither wanted to be slowed down, certainly not for anything as prosaic as air. Carrie's hands roamed over him, tugging his dark cotton shirt from the waistband of his cutoff jeans, and then slipping beneath the material to feel the bare, muscled warmth of his back.

She felt his lips nibbling an erotic trail along the sensitive curve of her neck, and her legs seemed to liquefy, leaving her weak and clinging to him for support. A long shudder ran through her and she pressed closer, nuzzling against him, her surrender complete.

"I wanted you for so long," she murmured achingly. "I think about you every day, every night.... When you left tonight, I—"

"I didn't want to go," he said huskily. His mouth poised over hers and he gazed deeply into her passion-drugged eyes. "I couldn't stay away, Carrie." His thumb traced the sweet fullness of her lower lip and she shivered at the small, sensual caress. Desire shot through him like a hot spear. "I want to make love to you, Carrie. If I have to wait any longer, I—"

"No." She laid her fingers gently across his lips, hushing him. "No more waiting, Tyler. I love you so much. I want to show you, I want you to—"

Tyler groaned her name and kissed her, lingeringly, deeply. The kiss burned with all the passion and fire of their earlier kisses but contained a tenderness that rendered it sweeter and more meaningful.

Carrie writhed sinuously as his big hands moved over her, molding the blue silk of her nightshirt against her skin. She felt the warming heat of his palms through the cloth, and then on her bare skin itself, as he slowly and sensuously stroked the smooth skin of her thighs.

She kissed him back desperately, drunk on the taste and the scent of him, wanting him with a fierce primal need that she had never before experienced. When his hand slipped from behind to probe between her parted legs, she gasped at the audacious caress. But she wanted it, wanted it....

Moaning, she squeezed her eyes shut and clung to him as his fingers slid over the cotton-and-lace barrier of her panties, back and forth, slowly, lightly, before he finally slipped beneath to touch her creamy, swollen center.

"Tyler," she begged in a soft, shaky voice. Excitement throbbed deliciously in the dark, secret core of her, spreading an aching tension to every sensual zone in her body. Her body pressed against his hand as she gave herself up to the voluptuous pleasure he was building.

It took an act of will for Tyler to rein himself in, to remove his hand and hold her slightly away from him. "Sweetheart, not here," he said raspily. "I don't want our first time together to be in the hall!"

"I don't care where we are, I just want you," she murmured dreamily.

The sight of Carrie's face, tilted back, her cheeks flushed with color, her mouth soft and moist and rosy from his kisses, those beautiful blue eyes of hers dark with passion, sent another stunning bolt of desire through him. He lifted her in his arms, holding her high against his chest.

Though he had never said the words "I love you" to any woman—there were certain lines that even Tyler Tremaine didn't cross—he had never been closer to saying them than he was right now as he stood holding Carrie in his arms. "Let me take you to bed," he whispered instead.

"Yes," Carrie agreed softly, caressing his face with her fingertips. She traced his cheekbones, the strong curve of his jaw, feeling overwhelmed by the sweet, sensuous emotions surging through her. "Yes, love."

He strode swiftly up the stairs, past the partially closed door of the triplets' room, where they lay sleeping quietly inside. Sleuth, the cat, was stretched luxuriously across Carrie's bed, and the sight of the big striped cat made both Carrie and Tyler smile.

"I'll let you escort him out," Tyler said, setting Carrie on her feet. "Old Psycho-Kitty already holds a world-class grudge against me."

"Nonsense. You're just imagining it," Carrie assured him as she lifted the cat from the bed. She put him in the hall, and the cat sauntered off with a haughty meow, as if it was his idea to leave in the first place. "Sleuth likes you, Tyler."

"Yeah, I can tell how much he likes me by the way he bares his fangs and hisses at me whenever I come near him. I appeal to him about as much as—uh—wolverines appeal to me."

Their eyes met and they grinned at each other. Tyler reached out and took both her hands in his, his expression sobering, his voice deep and low. "Carrie, I just want you to know that I would never use you or deliberately hurt you or humiliate you. That scene tonight at my father's house was—"

"It's over and done with," Carrie said quietly. "It was a misunderstanding." Her lips quirked into a playful smile.

"But I have a feeling we'll be long remembered out there. The kids and I did make a lasting first impression."

"You certainly made a lasting first impression on me. I haven't been able to get you out of my head since I met you." Still holding her hands, Tyler jerked her toward him. When her body impacted against his, they embraced, melding together with a long, mutual sigh. They held each other tightly, savoring their closeness.

The fiery passion between them, never far beneath the surface, flared like a spark to tinder. Their lips met and clung, their hands feverishly caressing. Carrie could feel every hard line of his body against her softer, yielding flesh, and she moaned and moved suggestively, wanting to offer him an unmistakable invitation.

It was one Tyler was eagerly willing to accept. Pausing to kiss her again and again, he walked her backward to the bed. They sank down onto the mattress, kissing with hungry desperation, their bodies stretched out and intertwined and radiating sensual heat.

Carrie felt his fingers on the top button of her nightshirt, and she drew in a sharp, shaky breath. He performed the task with such deft swiftness that she scarcely had time to exhale before he had unfastened every button and was opening the folds of silk. He slipped the garment from her shoulders and tossed it aside. Deep within her, the coil of desire tightened. There was something so sexy about his urgency and his directness. He wanted her, and he was making sure she knew how much.

She gazed at him, watching him as he stared at her naked breasts for the first time. "Do you know how many times I've dreamed of seeing you this way?" he murmured huskily. "Both at night and during the day." He touched the underside of her breast with his long fingers, then began to knead her soft breasts, plumping their roundness in his hands and gliding his thumbs over the rigid tips.

"I wondered about what color your nipples were." He bent his head and traced the dark pink bud with the tip of his tongue. "I tried to imagine their size and shape." He treated her other nipple to the same arousing treatment. "But my imagination didn't come close to visualizing how beautiful you really are, Carrie. How perfect."

Carrie's body pulsed with a pleasurable tension that kept building and growing with his every word, his every touch. She cried out his name, lost in the magic of the sensual spell Tyler was weaving.

He drew her nipple into his mouth and sucked strongly. Carrie almost sobbed as an electric spasm of pleasure streaked through her. The sensations he was evoking were wild and overwhelming, and the hot throbbing between her legs intensified. She wriggled restlessly, seeking to assuage the ache. In response to her silent plea, Tyler placed his big, warm hand exactly where she most wanted it.

He could feel the dewy moisture there, and the evidence of her deep feminine arousal excited him even more. Stripping off her panties with one deft sweep, he penetrated her hot silken softness gently with his fingers as his tongue, deep in her mouth, was thrusting in deep, sure strokes.

The potent dual mastery evoked an intense, incredible pleasure that rocketed through her with a swift, surging force that suddenly, wildly exploded within her. Radiant waves of heat rolled through her, pulsing through her body and bathing her in a warm, glowing sea.

Her release made her limp and pliant, and for a moment, she lay still on the bed, breathing deeply, her eyes closed. Tyler lay beside her, his hands moving possessively over her in long, lazy caresses.

Carrie opened her eyes and looked into his. They smiled, naturally, simultaneously. The emotional bond that had grown and strengthened between them these past weeks was too deep to allow any awkwardness between them.

"Why have we waited so long for something that is so right?" Tyler asked wryly, kissing her cheek.

"It's right because we waited so long," Carrie said logically.

She gazed at him, her blue eyes shining. A wonderful, powerful rush of love poured through her and it was no longer enough that she lay here passively, luxuriating in her own blissful languor. She wanted to give him pleasure, to take him into her, joining their bodies together. She already felt the power of their emotional and spiritual connection; a physical union would truly make them one.

Carrie touched him, her slender hands moving over him with loving boldness, slipping under his shirt to explore the wiry mat of hair on his chest and following it as it arrowed downward, beyond the waistband of his jeans. Her thumb dipped into the circle of his navel, tracing its shape.

She loved having unlimited access to his body, touching him the way she'd been yearning to for so long. But his clothes were definitely a barrier, one she intended to quickly dispose of. Her fingers tugged at the thick metal buttons of his fly, but she prevailed over each one. Tyler made an inarticulate sound as she boldly slipped her hand inside to take possession of him.

He allowed her to fondle him for a few ecstatic moments, then caught her hands, stilling them. "Any more of that and I'll go completely over the edge."

"Good." Carrie nearly purred with pure feminine satisfaction. "I want you to, Tyler."

He managed a hoarse laugh. "But not quite yet. Carrie, about protection..."

Her eyes widened. "Uh-oh. I don't have anything, Tyler. There's been no reason for it," she added meaningfully.

"I know. Not to worry." He reached into the pocket of his jeans. "I came prepared," he said, triumphantly pulling out a foil packet.

Carrie sat up. "You were very confident, weren't you?"

"Believe me, baby, I had to be. I've never been so desperate or so unglued in my entire life." He stripped off his clothes as he spoke.

Carrie opened the packet. "So you brought this one."

He pulled three more from his pockets. "I thought about showing up with the entire box of twenty-four but . . ." His voice trailed off. Carrie was laughing, and he joined in, feeling happier and freer and more lighthearted than he'd ever felt.

He pulled her down to him. "Carrie," he said urgently. His control was rapidly dissolving. Feeling her warm, eager body in his arms, her lips grazing his skin, her hands reaching for him, was too much for him to resist.

There was no need to resist. She wanted him as much as he wanted her, and the reasons they had come up with to stay apart seemed inconsequential and meaningless. The only thing that mattered was the two of them together at last, giving in to the powerful feelings they had for each other.

They had both reached their limit, and when Carrie's legs opened to him, welcoming him into her dark soft heat, Tyler drove into her with an urgent, powerful thrust. For a moment, they lay motionless as they gazed into each other's eyes, acknowledging that her body enveloped his, and that something between them had irrevocably been changed forever.

The indescribable pleasure of their mating consumed them both, and they moved together in a passionate frenzy, the sensual fire flaming to white-hot intensity, until both were seared by the sheer heat of the pleasure coursing through them.

Their wild urgency further incited them. Carrie felt his body surge to completion deep within her, and it triggered her own release. She cried out Tyler's name as her body shook with the pulsing satisfaction that swept her away on waves of rapture.

They spent the rest of the night together, turning to each other again and again, as if neither could quite believe that the waiting and the loneliness were over, that they could touch and kiss each other freely, at will. That they could satiate the burning desire that even the simplest touch or kiss evoked within them.

Finally, deliciously languid and sated, Carrie's eyes drifted closed, and she cuddled back into Tyler, her mind floating dreamily. He fit his body to hers like a spoon and closed his arms around her.

She sighed blissfully. "What are you thinking, Tyler?" she murmured drowsily, exhausted but still unable to break their connection, even to sleep.

Tyler smiled in the darkness. "That now I don't have to come up with a scheme to get you into my bed when we go to the beach this weekend."

She chuckled softly. "Was that your plan?"

His reply was heartfelt. "Oh, yeah!"

"And now you think I'll hop into bed with you the minute we get the kids tucked in?"

"We'll wait till we're sure they're asleep," Tyler corrected. "Then we'll hop into bed."

She laid her hands over his, interlacing their fingers. "I can't wait."

Moments later, they were both asleep.

Eleven

Their weekend trip to the beach was a weekend of firsts. Carrie and Tyler's first as a couple. The triplets' first long car ride and their first sojourn away from home. And the first time that all five were away and out together as a family.

That was the way everybody saw them, as a mother and father with their three small children. Tyler was astounded by the number of comments the sight of the triplets evoked from strangers. He lost count of the people who came up to them, asking the children's age and all sorts of information about them.

Carrie, who'd grown up a triplet, was used to it. "The curiosity levels off when they get older and don't look the same age and so much alike."

Tyler vicariously enjoyed the attention the children drew. He was proud of them and enjoyed talking about them. And he didn't once correct the misapprehension that he was the daddy in the group.

It was fun introducing the children to the beach and the ocean, to see the wonderment in their eyes as they saw the waves break and ebb, to hold their small hands as the water rushed around their ankles while they shrieked with delight. The water-loving trio had no fear of the ocean—just the opposite, in fact. Carrie and Tyler had to watch them closely to keep them from dashing headlong into the surf.

Playing in the sand was one of the children's favorite pastimes, and the beach, so impressively larger than their sandpile at home, enthralled all three. The wide assortment of sand toys that Tyler purchased at the local old-style five-and-dime store kept them occupied for hours.

At Tyler's insistence, they ate all their meals in restaurants, child-friendly ones. The kiddie pavilion, filled with toddler-sized rides, was another treat. Tyler and Carrie stood with the other parents and waved as the children rode the tiny boats and cars and airplanes around and around.

Dylan, Emily and Franklin were euphoric but exhausted when Tyler and Carrie finally tucked them into their rented cribs. That was when the focus of the brief vacation abruptly shifted to become strictly adult-oriented. After closing the door to the children's room, Tyler scooped up Carrie in his arms and carried her to his bedroom.

"I had a great time with the kids today, but every time I looked at you, I got hard, wanting you," he confessed huskily, as he swiftly divested her of her sky-blue shorts and top. Her underwear immediately joined the small heap of clothes, his and hers, on the floor beside the bed.

His hands flexed on her waist, then moved up to cup her rounded bare breasts. "I want you so much, Carrie. I can't stop thinking about how good it felt to be inside you."

Carrie reached out to intimately caress him, feeling his hard, male response and glorying in her feminine power to please him. "Make love to me, Tyler," she whispered impassionedly.

His mouth covered hers and her arms went around his neck to draw him closer. Their kiss was long and slow and deep. They wanted to take their time, to make it last, but the rush of passion was fast and hot and overwhelming. They fell onto the bed, hot and tangled together, kissing and caressing in a feverish frenzy of desire.

Tyler positioned himself intimately between her thighs, and Carrie arched up to accept him, wrapping her legs around him and sobbing his name as he surged into her. He heaved a groan of ecstasy as he thrust deeper into her moist warmth, muffling the noise against her neck.

They moved together in wild primal rhythm, the intense pleasure building until the erotic flames engulfed them and they exploded into a searing, simultaneous climax.

Afterward, they lay together, relaxed and drained and wonderfully content.

"I could get addicted to this," Carrie confessed softly, nestling her head in the hollow of his shoulder. "I love you, Tyler."

Tyler pulled her closer and kissed the top of her head, his lips lingering to caress her silky blond hair. He knew that he was already addicted, but he felt no compunction to tell her so. Cautious bachelor habits die hard; he was not about to blurt out his feelings, to tell her *everything*. They had plenty of time. He would take things slowly, see where it all led.

"We're great together in bed," he said with a satisfied sigh. Some things were self-evident and safe enough to reveal.

"We're great together out of bed, too," Carrie said softly. She was aching for him to tell her that he loved her. And she knew instinctively that he wasn't going to say the words, that he was holding back. It was maddening. How long was he going to insist on playing it cool? He certainly wanted her and not just for sex. Carrie was sure she meant more to him than that. She would bet her house that he loved her children.

But her knowing all of this and him admitting it were two different things. She wondered how long it would take for their separate perceptions to converge. Weeks, months, *years?* For the first time since she'd made love with Tyler, Carrie allowed herself to think of Ian and their short, tragic relationship. How fortunate that she and Ian hadn't wasted any time deciding how they felt about each other! They'd committed themselves and forged ahead, without knowing how little time they would actually have together.

She had learned an invaluable lesson there: that time was fleeting and there were no guarantees. It had been wrong to deny her feelings for Tyler simply because she feared the pain of losing him. Fighting the need to love to avoid being hurt was both tragic and foolish, she realized now.

All those games and attitudes that kept lovers apart wasted precious time, and it was a loss that could never be regained. A couple should joyfully acknowledge their love and openly celebrate it. Carrie sighed softly. If only Tyler shared her hard-found beliefs.

Tyler heard her sigh. "Are you all right?" he asked, tightening his arms possessively around her. He'd been pretty wild, taking her with an urgency that he suddenly feared might have been too rough for her. She was so small and delicate, so utterly feminine. "Carrie, did I hurt you?" His voice deepened with concern.

"I'm fine," she said warmly, leaning up to kiss him. "Better than fine. I feel wonderful. I—I was just thinking about—" She paused and gulped for breath. She didn't want any secrets between them. "About Ian."

"Ian wouldn't begrudge you getting on with your life, Carrie," Tyler said quickly. *He was not going to lose Carrie to Ian Wilcox's ghost, not now!* "From what I've heard about him, he would want you to—love me."

Carrie nodded. Ian had been a generous young man who definitely would have wanted his wife to love again. An ironic little smile curved her lips. She suspected, however, that Ian would've wanted the man she loved to return her love in full measure. To hold back nothing and not choke on the words.

It was nearly nine o'clock on Sunday night when the group returned to the city, their weekend idyll ended. The children were asleep in their car seats, and Carrie and Tyler glanced back at them, then at each other.

"I don't want it to be over," Carrie said wistfully. "Back to having you in one house, me in another."

Tyler frowned. The arrangement sounded intolerable to him, too. "There's really no reason why I can't spend the night with you tonight. I'll get up a little earlier in the morning than usual and go back to my place to—"

He was interrupted by an abrupt, hard rap on the windshield. Alexa stood outside the car, gesturing to them, her blue eyes wide. Tyler swiftly rolled down the window. "What's up?" he asked, trying not to groan, for behind Alexa came Ben, sauntering down the walk. It appeared that it would be a while before he had Carrie all to himself again.

"Alexa, what's going on?" Carrie asked worriedly. She hadn't expected to find her sister and brother here; they knew she'd been away with Tyler.

"Mom and Dad are here, Carrie," Alexa whispered. "They arrived this morning from Germany, and they're—"

She didn't have a chance to finish. Colonel and Mrs. Shaw were hurrying toward them. Startled, Carrie hopped out of the car and rushed to meet her parents. Tyler climbed out and leaned against the side of the car, watching her.

"It's so good to see you!" Carrie exclaimed, hugging first her mother, then her father. "But what are you doing here?" She couldn't imagine what, if anything, could be wrong since everyone was present and appeared to be in the bloom of health, but she asked, anyway. "Is something wrong?"

"Nothing's wrong, except we missed you and our precious babies terribly, Carrie," her mother said tearfully. "Oh, I have to see them! Alexa, Ben, help me get them out of their car seats."

Tyler thought of his and Carrie's plans to carefully spirit each sleeping child from car to crib without awakening them, thus giving themselves a quiet, private evening alone together. With the additional cast of characters, who were now holding the very wide-awake toddlers, the sexy evening he had anticipated was currently outside the realm of possibility. Tyler heaved a quiet sigh of regret.

The fond grandmother, Alexa and Ben quickly disappeared inside the house with the triplets, leaving Carrie and Tyler alone with Colonel Shaw. Tyler studied the older man, who was tall, fair and blue-eyed and maintained the erect posture and carriage of a military officer.

"We missed you, Carrie." The colonel hugged his daughter affectionately, his voice warm. "Your mom and I have been—"

"Daddy, I want you to meet a—uh—a good friend of mine," Carrie cut in quickly, her eyes connecting with Tyler's. "This is Tyler Tremaine," she said, leaving her father's embrace to extend her hand to Tyler. She didn't get close enough to reach him. The colonel put his arm around her shoulders and kept her in place by his side. Carrie merely smiled. "Tyler, this is my father, Colonel Shaw. I'd've introduced you to my mother but she seems to have disappeared."

"She couldn't wait to get her hands on our grandbabies again," the colonel explained indulgently. He glanced briefly at Tyler. "I believe you're Carrie's next-door neighbor, hmm? Alexa mentioned you. You drove Carrie and the children to the shore this weekend, I hear."

Tyler frowned. Stated like that, his ties to Carrie and the triplets sounded tenuous and so very casual. *A neighbor who'd driven them to the shore?* Clearly, the colonel wasn't getting the true picture here. Tyler cleared his throat. "Yes, but we've—"

"I want to thank you for being such a good neighbor to my daughter and my grandchildren," Colonel Shaw cut in, his tone unmistakably commanding. "But it's a role you will no longer have to play. My wife and I are here to take Carrie and the children back to Germany with us."

"What?" Carrie and Tyler chorused together.

Colonel Shaw turned away from Tyler, focusing his attention on his daughter. "Carrie, my dear, I realize that I made a terrible mistake, encouraging you to stay alone here in the city with the babies. I thought I was acting in your best interests but—"

"I know you were, Dad," Carrie interjected and earned a disapproving frown from her father for the interruption.

"Carrie, I was wrong," he insisted. "And when I'm wrong, I prefer to admit it rather than continue to support a fallacious decision. Your mother and I have both been so worried about you and the children, with the two of us so far away and unable to help you. It's intolerable! We're taking you all back with us."

"Daddy, we're fine!" Carrie said exasperatedly. "Honestly, you have no reason to worry about us."

"Your hours at the hospital are long and exhausting, and then you have to come home to three toddlers who demand your constant care and attention," Colonel Shaw intoned firmly. "I know what I said about you working, but again, I was wrong. It's more important for you to spend your time and energy on your children, Carrie."

"I know the hours are long, but I've been handling it, Dad," Carrie insisted. "And the kids are fine when I'm gone. Alexa stays with them and—"

"Which brings us to another point that has your mother worried sick," the colonel boomed. "Your sister has become a recluse. From what we've gleaned, Alexa has no social life whatsoever. She spends every single weekend taking care of your children and hiding from the world in general.''

"Daddy!" Carrie protested impatiently.

"All right, we won't get into that now. We'll get back to the main issue at hand, and that is you and your children. I firmly believe that they need you—their mother!—with them full-time.''

"We agree on that point, Colonel Shaw," Tyler said, nodding his affirmation.

The colonel glanced at Tyler, as if surprised to still see him there. "Interesting," he said, polite but brisk. "Feel free to leave at any time, Mr. Tremaine. I'm sure you're eager to be on your way. This is really no concern of yours, after all. Mrs. Shaw and I will carry on from here."

Tyler gaped at the colonel. *He'd been dismissed!* Ordered to leave like a low-ranking young airman sent off to KP duty or whatever low-ranking young airmen were ordered to do by their superior officers.

Colonel Shaw, his arm firmly around Carrie's shoulders, was hurrying her toward the house, talking all the way. "We have a four-bedroom house on base, Carrie, with one of the bedrooms plenty big enough for the triplets and all their things. And since we're right on the base, it'll be easy for you to get out with the children. The three of them are getting older now, Carrie, and it's important to get them out and about, to see new things and meet new people. Mom and I are hoping to talk Alexa into coming over and living with us, too. She needs a change of scene or she'll never get out of the rut she's fallen into. I happen to have several very fine young pilots in my squadron, and I'm looking forward to introducing them to both you and your sister..."

They disappeared into the house, and the front door banged shut. Tyler stood alone in the front yard, staring at the closed door, the colonel's resonant tones still ringing in his ears.

He was confused, almost disoriented. Everything had happened with such speed, he was still having trouble processing it all. Moments before, he had been planning to spend the night with his lover. Now she'd been whisked away from him by her father—*who planned to take her and the babies to live in Germany!*

Just for a moment, Tyler allowed himself to consider his life with Carrie and the children no longer in it. He found himself facing a dark abyss of loneliness that was so terrible and so soul-shattering that he immediately rebelled against it.

He stormed to the front door and started pounding on it.

"Door's open! Come in!" Mrs. Shaw called cheerfully.

Tyler accepted the invitation and strode into the kitchen where the colonel and his wife and both sets of triplets, adult and children, were gathered.

"Carrie, I want to talk to you," Tyler said forcefully, every bit the executive heir apparent. "And you, too, Colonel," he added, his tone making it clear that he was no junior featherweight to be fobbed off.

He snatched Carrie's hand and half dragged her into the living room. Colonel Shaw followed a few paces behind, his expression enigmatic.

"Colonel Shaw, first of all, I want you to know that I'm not merely a neighbor of your daughter's," Tyler declared, meeting the older man's eyes challengingly. He pulled Carrie back against him, wrapping his arms around her and locking his hands to rest possessively on her stomach.

"Carrie, we owe it to your father to be honest with him. And before anything else is said, before things get even more out of hand, I'm telling you that you are *not* going to Germany with your parents."

"Well now, Mr. Tremaine, that's a bit presumptuous of you, isn't it?" Colonel Shaw drawled. "I think that's a decision that Carrie has to make herself. She has to consider her options, her children being her first priority."

Carrie looked hard at her father. There was something in his tone, something in his eyes...something undefinable that someone who didn't know the colonel as well as she did would miss completely. Something was going on here.... When she saw Ben lurking beyond the threshold, she was certain of it. Her brows narrowed. "Daddy, what are you and—"

"Carrie, I—I—I love you," Tyler burst out, knocking her conspiracy theory right out of her mind. "I will *not* let you go halfway around the world, and I won't let you take the kids away. They're *my* kids, too, Carrie! I love them and they love me—they're mine in every way that counts, and so are you. You belong to me, Carrie, and you know it as well as I do. We're—" He paused and drew a deep breath. "We're going to get married—as soon as possible."

The moment he said the words, he realized just how much he meant them. Marrying Carrie, raising the triplets, was exactly what he wanted to do. He just hadn't let himself think that far ahead before. Now that he had, he was chomping at the bit to begin his new life with them.

"Well," Colonel Shaw smiled broadly. "That certainly puts this matter in an entirely different perspective." He turned and found himself face-to-face with an exultant Ben, who'd been shamelessly eavesdropping. "I think we'll give Carrie and Tyler some time alone, son. Let's give Mom and Alexa a hand with the little ones." Ben let out an exuberant cheer, and the colonel swiftly hustled him out.

Tyler turned Carrie in his arms. His own smile was as wide as Ben's and his green eyes were glittering with triumph. *Carrie and the children were his!* He couldn't ever remember feeling this happy—not even when he was named executive vice-president, the position that put him on the track to the company presidency. This was a kind of euphoria he had never known, an all-consuming joy that touched his heart and soul and sent his spirit soaring.

He bent his head, eager to claim a kiss from his wife-to-be, but when his mouth sought hers, it collided instead with her fingers, which she'd placed against his lips. "Tyler, I can't let you go through with this," she said, her blue eyes bright with unshed tears. "You—you don't have to marry me to keep me from taking the kids to Germany. Before you came in, I'd already told my parents that I had no intention of leaving. We're staying here."

"Carrie, I asked you to marry me," Tyler said urgently. It suddenly occurred to him that she hadn't accepted his proposal—the first marriage proposal he'd ever made to anyone. "You love me, Carrie. You and I both know it. And I love you." It was easier to say the second time. So easy that he said it again. "I love you, and we both know that, too. I want to marry you and adopt the kids. I want the five of us to be a family."

"Tyler, you don't understand," Carrie whispered, trying to swallow the emotional sob welling up within her. "I'm afraid you were tricked into proposing to me. They haven't confirmed it yet, but I'm willing to bet that Ben had something to do with getting Mom and Dad over here. I don't know what he told them, but I'm positive that this visit and their sudden insistence on taking the babies and me to Germany has something to do with wringing a commitment out of you."

"And it worked!" Tyler broke into laughter. He was too happy to do anything else. "It seems I've seriously underestimated your brother Ben. He has the savvy and the skills and creative killer instinct that Tremaine Incorporated looks for in advertising. I'll have to look over his ideas, maybe offer him a job—after our wedding, of course."

"Oh, Tyler!" Tears of joy streamed down Carrie's cheeks. She linked her arms around his neck and gazed up at him, all her love shining in her beautiful blue eyes. "I love you so and I want to marry you, but I don't want you to ever feel you've been manipulated."

Tyler groaned impatiently. "Are you going to say you'll marry me, or am I going to have to get down on bended knee and propose the old-fashioned way? Because I'll do whatever it takes to convince you that I want you to be my wife, Carrie. I want you more than anything in the world."

His lips touched hers, lightly at first, then with increasing, erotic pressure. "And if you're willing to brave another pregnancy, I'd love to have a child with you."

"According to our family history, there is every chance that *a* child might be twins or even another set of triplets," she warned.

"Hey, I'm game if you are. We'll talk about it again in a few years, when the triple treat are approaching school age, okay?"

"Okay. And, Tyler, one more thing."

"For you, anything, my love."

"Don't you think it's time to bury the hatchet with your father and Nina? To get to know your half brother and to trust him when he says he's not out to steal your job or your position in the family? Because I don't think he is, Tyler. I think he wants your friendship."

Tyler considered it. "He did volunteer to chase you for me on the Fourth of July." He grinned, remembering the end of the chase. "And look where we ended up after that."

"With a happy ending," said Carrie, smiling radiantly.

"Not to mention, in bed. Which is where we're going right now, to my place, where we can be alone. I think we have enough baby-sitters over here to cover our absence."

"I know we do," Carrie said, kissing him with all the love and passion she felt for him.

Tyler picked her up and carried her out the door, through the gap in the hedge to his house, where they spent the night celebrating their love.

*   *   *   *   *

INTIMATE MOMENTS®
10TH
Anniversary

Celebrate our anniversary with a fabulous collection of firsts....

The first Intimate Moments titles written by three of your favorite authors:

NIGHT MOVES   **Heather Graham Pozzessere**
LADY OF THE NIGHT **Emilie Richards**
A STRANGER'S SMILE **Kathleen Korbel**

Silhouette Intimate Moments is proud to present a FREE hardbound collection of our authors' firsts—titles that you will treasure in the years to come, from some of the line's founding writers.

This collection will not be sold in retail stores and is available only through this exclusive offer. Look for details in Silhouette Intimate Moments titles available in retail stores in May, June and July.

SIMANNR

OFFICIAL RULES • MILLION DOLLAR BIG WIN SWEEPSTAKES
NO PURCHASE OR OBLIGATION NECESSARY TO ENTER

To enter, follow the directions published. **ALTERNATE MEANS OF ENTRY:** Hand-print your name and address on a 3″×5″ card and mail to either: Silhouette Big Win, 3010 Walden Ave., P.O. Box 1867, Buffalo, NY 14269-1867, or Silhouette Big Win, P.O. Box 609, Fort Erie, Ontario L2A 5X3, and we will assign your Sweepstakes numbers (Limit: one entry per envelope). For eligibility, entries must be received no later than March 31, 1994 and be sent via 1st-class mail. No liability is assumed for printing errors or lost, late or misdirected entries.

To determine winners, the sweepstakes numbers on submitted entries will be compared against a list of randomly preselected prizewinning numbers. In the event all prizes are not claimed via the return of prizewinning numbers, random drawings will be held from among all other entries received to award unclaimed prizes.

Prizewinners will be determined no later than May 30, 1994. Selection of winning numbers and random drawings are under the supervision of D.L. Blair, Inc., an independent judging organization whose decisions are final. One prize to a family or organization. No substitution will be made for any prize, except as offered. Taxes and duties on all prizes are the sole responsibility of winners. Winners will be notified by mail. Chances of winning are determined by the number of entries distributed and received.

Sweepstakes open to persons 18 years of age or older, except employees and immediate family members of Torstar Corporation, D.L. Blair, Inc., their affiliates, subsidiaries and all other agencies, entities and persons connected with the use, marketing or conduct of this Sweepstakes. All applicable laws and regulations apply. Sweepstakes offer void wherever prohibited by law. Any litigation within the province of Quebec respecting the conduct and awarding of a prize in this Sweepstakes must be submitted to the Régies des Loteries et Courses du Quebec. In order to win a prize, residents of Canada will be required to correctly answer a time-limited arithmetical skill-testing question. Values of all prizes are in U.S. currency.

Winners of major prizes will be obligated to sign and return an affidavit of eligibility and release of liability within 30 days of notification. In the event of non-compliance within this time period, prize may be awarded to an alternate winner. Any prize or prize notification returned as undeliverable will result in the awarding of the prize to an alternate winner. By acceptance of their prize, winners consent to use of their names, photographs or other likenesses for purposes of advertising, trade and promotion on behalf of Torstar Corporation without further compensation, unless prohibited by law.

This Sweepstakes is presented by Torstar Corporation, its subsidiaries and affiliates in conjunction with book, merchandise and/or product offerings. Prizes are as follows: Grand Prize—$1,000,000 (payable at $33,333.33 a year for 30 years). First through Sixth Prizes may be presented in different creative executions, each with the following approximate values: First Prize—$35,000; Second Prize—$10,000; 2 Third Prizes—$5,000 each; 5 Fourth Prizes—$1,000 each; 10 Fifth Prizes—$250 each; 1,000 Sixth Prizes—$100 each. Prizewinners will have the opportunity of selecting any prize offered for that level. A travel-prize option if offered and selected by winner, must be completed within 12 months of selection and is subject to hotel and flight accommodations availability. Torstar Corporation may present this sweepstakes utilizing names other than Million Dollar Sweepstakes. For a current list of all prize options offered within prize levels and all names the Sweepstakes may utilize, send a self-addressed stamped envelope (WA residents need not affix return postage) to: Million Dollar Sweepstakes Prize Options/Names, P.O. Box 7410, Blair, NE 68009.

For a list of prizewinners (available after July 31, 1994) send a separate, stamped self-addressed envelope to: Million Dollar Sweepstakes Winners, P.O. Box 4728, Blair NE 68009.

SWPS693

SILHOUETTE® Desire®

THEY'RE HOT...
THEY'RE COOL...
THEY'RE ALL-AMERICAN GUYS...
THEY'RE RED, WHITE AND BLUE HEROES

Zeke #793 by Annette Broadrick *(Man of the Month)*
Ben #794 by Karen Leabo
Derek #795 by Leslie Davis Guccione
Cameron #796 by Beverly Barton
Jake #797 by Helen R. Myers
Will #798 by Kelly Jamison

Look for these six red-blooded, white-knight, blue-collar men
Coming your way next month
Only from Silhouette Desire

Relive the romance...
Harlequin and Silhouette
are proud to present

A program of collections of three complete novels by the most requested authors with the most requested themes. Be sure to look for one volume each month with three complete novels by top name authors.

In June: **NINE MONTHS** Penny Jordan
Stella Cameron
Janice Kaiser

Three women pregnant and alone. But a lot can happen in nine months!

In July: **DADDY'S HOME** Kristin James
Naomi Horton
Mary Lynn Baxter

Daddy's Home ... and his presence is long overdue!

In August: **FORGOTTEN PAST** Barbara Kaye
Pamela Browning
Nancy Martin

Do you dare to create a future if you've forgotten the past?

Available at your favorite retail outlet.

◆ HARLEQUIN®   ▼ Silhouette